The Missionary

A STORY THE OPPOSITE OF KIERKEGAARD'S

JON FERGUSON

Huge Jam Publishing
2024

Copyright © 2024 Jon Ferguson

ISBN: 978-1-916604-25-4

CONTENTS

ONE

EDGAR GOES TO CHURCH AND THINKS ABOUT HIS NAME

God. Odg. Ogd. Dog. Gdo. Dgo. After a few seconds Edgar-In-Church was quite certain these were the only possible combinations of the three letters. God and dog were the only ones that felt like English. The others looked African or Swedish or something. He didn't write the possibilities out until he got home later that day. Later was three church meetings later which would put the clock at about three in the afternoon. The baseball game on TV would be almost over unless it was a high scoring affair or went into extra innings. The Giants were in Los Angeles and game time was one p.m.

Edgar-In-Church wasn't really named Edgar-In-Church except by himself and only then when he was in church. Otherwise his name was Edgar which gave him these possibilities (as he figured out later that same day): Darge, Garde, Aedrg, Agedr, Gaerd, Radeg, Raged, Eragd, Egadr, Adreg, Agred, Regad, Ragde, Dgrea, Dearg, Darag, Drgea, Deagr, Gared, Geard, Gdrea, Gedar, Gread, Aedgr. There had to be more he knew, but these are the ones he wrote out on the sheet of paper under the God-Odg-Ogd-Dog-Dgo-Odg ones. He thought his parents probably chose the letters first, i. e. A D E G R, then they mixed them like he had done and settled on Edgar. He would have chosen Geard, he thought, or maybe Darge, but not Edgar. For him, all the names that started with vowels looked a little weaker than the consonant-starting ones. He didn't know why, but they did. Vowel-starting names, he thought, were for girls. Names like Edith or Alice or Arabella.

Back in church that morning he wondered who gave God His name. Maybe He gave it to Himself, in which case Edgar thought he should have been able to choose his own appellation as well. But then if somebody else gave God His name, Edgar decided he had no complaint. But who could have named God? Did he have a mother and father? Edgar had heard the word "Godfather" before, so maybe that was the guy who named the Almighty. But then, Edgar reasoned with his twelve-year-old brain, a guy who was almighty surely wouldn't let someone else name him. He wouldn't take any chances on getting a name he didn't like. Like Edgar. Actually, as he sat in the second church meeting that morning, he decided God was a strange name because it didn't have a last name. God McCormick would have been okay (Mike McCormick was scheduled to pitch for the Giants). God Mays or God McCovey made more sense too. God Cepeda sounded good. So did God

Davenport. God Marichal sounded the best. So why hadn't anybody done anything to fix the problem? Oh well, he thought as he hummed along with the closing song of the second meeting:

Onward Christian soldiers
Marching off to war
With a cross of Jesus
Going on before

Edgar had always noticed that "Onward Christian Soldiers" was one of the tunes the congregation sang the loudest. They sang "Love at Home" loudly, too. The only song they probably sang louder than "Onward Christian Soldiers" was "The Spirit of God Like a Fire Is Burning". On thinking this, Edgar thought maybe God didn't have a last name because a song called "The Spirit of God McCormick Like a Fire is Burning" would have sounded lousy. As the people around him powered into the refrain for the second time, Edgar got goosebumps on his spine. They lasted about five seconds. After his back felt completely normal again, he wondered why Christians would go to war if the Bible said Thou Shalt Not Kill. As far as he knew, unless you were playing with green plastic soldiers, the object of war was to kill. But, hey, he had seen some of his church friends get whacked by their parents not too long after they'd been sitting together as a perfect family bellowing "LOVE AT HOME...LOVE

AT HOME" right there on the front row. So, after Edgar reflected Edgar-like, he decided the songs were meant to be sung and not lived. Or something like that.

The first meeting that day was called Priesthood Meeting and it was only for men and boys over twelve. It started at eight and Edgar rode with his father in their baby blue Plymouth with dark blue seats and enough room in the back to set up a card table. When they went to Priesthood Meeting, Edgar got to sit in the front seat with his dad because his mother and two sisters weren't there. They didn't have to go because they weren't men or boys. They came later for Sunday School in the second car, the Ford Falcon that always sounded like it wasn't going to make it up the hill to the chapel.

When Edgar sat in the front seat with his father he would either look out the window with difficulty because he was small or he would look at his father's nose. His father's nose was the only nose he knew that always looked broken. The top part went almost straight out, then it dropped off like it should have been a waterfall. But it was a nose, not a waterfall, and, the fact is, Edgar liked it. His own nose looked like a gum drop. He liked it, too, but for other reasons. The blue Plymouth had fish fins at the back that reminded Edgar of his father's nose because they were sort of the same shape. They just ran in a different direction.

When Edgar wasn't looking at his father's nose, but out the window, he mostly saw the sky because he was so low in the seat. On this day the heavens above Pleasant Hill were blue. That meant the game wouldn't be rained out which was the worst thing that could happen in Edgar's life. The game was in Los Angeles, four hundred miles to the south, but Edgar was sure the blue sky would stretch at least that far. Sometimes he was able to see treetops or telephone poles, but mostly the sky was the scenery during the ride to church. Edgar usually rode home with his mother in the Falcon because she wouldn't hang around and talk as long as his father would after the last meeting. That way, he had more of a chance of seeing the end of the baseball game. Sometimes his mother stopped for ice cream cones which was called the after-Sunday-School treat. The only other time Edgar got an ice cream cone was after the dentist. The ones after Sunday School were better because then his mouth didn't hurt, but they did delay getting home for the game.

The three Sunday meetings were: Priesthood Meeting, Sunday School, and Sacrament Meeting. Edgar and his father went to all three; his mother and sisters went to the last two. Sometimes Edgar listened and sometimes he didn't. There were distractions everywhere like trying to think of all the combinations of the letters G – O – D or Sister Marsing's dresses which always looked two sizes too big or wondering how the Giants were doing. His clothes were a distraction too because he had to wear a white shirt and tie. He wondered why none of the pictures of Jesus had Him in a tie. If Jesus didn't have to wear a tie, why did Edgar? Once he asked Sister Marsing and she said, "Because Jesus was the son of God." This, Edgar thought but didn't say, was a lousy answer because Sister Marsing herself was always saying that they were all God's children, and Edgar knew that would make him God's son just like Jesus. So if Jesus didn't have to wear a tie because He was the Son of God, then why did he? But then Edgar remembered that when they referred to Jesus, the "s" in "son" was capitalised, and when they referred to the boys in church, the "s" stayed small. Maybe that was what Sister Marsing meant. Then Edgar wondered why "sister" had a capital "s".

The fact was, Edgar liked baseball uniforms much better than he liked church uniforms, and he thought Jesus Himself would have looked better in a baseball outfit than the white sheet get-ups He always wore. He probably would have had to cut His beard and long hair because no baseball players had that stuff. But once He had done that, He probably would have looked as good as Mays did in a uniform. He imagined Jesus most likely would have been a pitcher or a first baseman. Centerfield was a possibility too, but given that He liked to talk a lot He would have needed to be around the infield. Catcher was definitely out because He was too skinny.

Anyway, Edgar wondered if these kinds of distractions were keeping him from absorbing the full impact of the Gospel. Maybe he wasn't properly tuned to God, which made him wonder if this might prevent him from going to Heaven. When he thought this, he asked Sister Marsing during the Sunday School lesson if they had baseball in Heaven. She said she doubted God played games. What does He do then? thought Edgar. Without games, Heaven would be a God-awful place. Especially without the game of baseball. When he asked Sister Marsing what God did if He didn't play games, she said He did the Lord's work. Edgar was never sure if the Lord was God, or if the Lord was Jesus, or maybe some combination of both. But be that as it may, he couldn't understand how a guy – a Guy who could do exactly what He wanted to do all day long because He was Almighty – would choose work over playing games.

He decided to ask.

"Sister Marsing, if God is All Powerful, why would He want to work instead of play?"

"Edgar, the Lord's work never ends."

"But why does He work?"

"Because He must take care of His children?"

"Why doesn't He get babysitters and stuff like that to take care of His children?"

"The Lord doesn't work that way."

"Why not, Sister Marsing?"

"Because the Lord's ways are not our ways."

"Then why do we go to church?"

"To learn the Lord's ways."

"But if His ways aren't our ways...?"

"Edgar, the Lord is a great mystery that earthly man

can't fathom."

"What does that mean?"

"It means that only when we enter the Kingdom of Heaven will we be able to understand the great glories of God."

"So then what are we trying to understand while we're here in church?"

"We're trying to get closer to the Lord."

"But if we can't understand Him, how can we get closer to Him?"

Sister Marsing didn't know what to say, so she said, "You'll understand these things when you're older."

On the way home from church that day, Edgar's mother took him and his two sisters for ice cream. He heard the end of the Giants-Dodgers game on the radio in the car as they licked their cones. The Dodger won 6-5. McCovey and Mays had both homered, but for naught.

TWO

Now here's this boy Edgar, a good kid by most standards with a nicely planted young brain, who, like millions of children the world round, innocently follows his parents – Sunday after Sunday after Sunday – to church. He sits through meeting after meeting with his twelve-year-old mixture of patience and restlessness and absorbs. He can't help but absorb, like a sponge cake that gets left outside in the rain. He will hear about Jesus and the Lord and the Gospel and God and good and evil and Heaven and Earth and spirit and soul and body and these words will be the rain that will flatten his sponge. Will they not be with him, indelibly, until he, like the cake, mushily mingles with the soft stuff of the earth? Though he can take Sister Marsing to task and ask good questions that she can't answer, will he ever break free from these categories that are built into his porous head? Will, for example, the idea of God follow Edgar to his last human breath? He will believe in God or he will not believe in God, but will this God always be an issue? Will he ever get to the state of the dog or the chimpanzee and be able to wander through life in a truly "godless" bliss, where all notion of God is utterly absent. Man probably lived for a few million years, before civilization got ahold of him, in this godless state. But since the invention of the toilet and the toothpick, he has plastered the planet with gods. And no matter how hard he and we may try, most of us can't get these mammoth nails out of our heads. Are we not slaves to our gods, nailed to their crosses? If Edgar stops believing in God, will he not continue to keep "God" in his vocabulary for as long as he lives?

Another problem Edgar will have is the truth business. Sunday after Sunday he hears church member after church member say: "I know the Church is true," or "I know beyond a shadow of doubt that this is the true Church," or "Brothers and sisters, I stand on my feet before you to bear witness that this is the one true Church." Already at twelve Edgar has this steel dichotomy "true-untrue" welded to his brain. And we mean welded. Will he ever get over trying to figure out if things are true or not true? Will he spend the rest of his life battling a notion that may well be absolute hogwash? For it may be that nothing is "true" or "untrue", but will Edgar be stuck on the train tracks of his civilization trying with all his little might to figure out where veracity lies? Will he seek truth, bless him, like a mouse seeking its way out of a cage with no doors? Bless him again, for he knoweth not what he doeth.

THREE

EDGAR LOSES INTEREST IN BASEBALL AND WANTS TO
SAVE THE WORLD

It came to pass that when Edgar turned eighteen he thought baseball was a waste of time. He might have gone on to be a professional player were it not for his religious education, but the Gospel got the best of him. After spending his junior high and high school years in a universe dedicated to the curveball, the fastball, the screwball, the knuckleball, and otherwise someway trying to finagle a kiss out of the girl-of-the-month, Edgar finally took his years of Sundays to heart: man, he now thought, should spend his life trying to save the world. Actually, he just put two and two together: Jesus's job was to save humanity; we should be like Jesus; therefore we should do what we can to save humanity.

His task was an interesting one given the size of humanity. But at age eighteen, Edgar was full of enthusiasm and optimism. If Jesus could do it, he could do it. Actually, Jesus hadn't done it, as was evidenced by world wars, car crashes, famines, murders, plane crashes, civil wars, slavery, lynchings, electrocutions, lesser wars, polio, apoplexy, strokes, syphilis, senility, etc. But Edgar, like most people, was prepared to ignore this, keeping hope and faith that one day paradise would be the earth.

The year was nineteen hundred and sixty-nine when he set about to save the world. He started by getting himself elected vice-president of the freshman class at his Christian university plugged between the Uinta mountains and Utah Lake. He had a budget and an office and his intention was to use all the money and manpower at his disposal to raise the underprivileged to the status of everybody else. First, he set up a clothing drive to provide garments for the N.A.A.C.P. in Mississippi. After a week, his office and apartment were both stacked to the ceiling with smelly old washed and unwashed apparel. His door-to-door recruits had been instructed to accept only clean usable holeless clothes, but invariably people got away with cleaning out their closets and hampers while Edgar's disciples waited patiently at their doors. It was hard to say no to giving, even when the giving was from the hamper rather than the heart. Edgar boxed all the stuff in cartons that he and his girlfriend Mary got at furniture stores, then shipped it all to a man he had talked to on the phone in Mississippi. After two months he still hadn't heard back from the man, so he tried to call him. He got someone on the other end of the line that sounded like he was in a tavern or a pool hall. The man said he had never heard of Edgar, his university, or of Edgar's clothes. Edgar never got any more news from Mississippi.

Next, Edgar, with Mary now as not only girlfriend, but as untiring assistant, unleashed a tutoring program for local high school students who had trouble with their A-B-Cs, their multiplication tables, and trying to remember what the capital of Delaware was. This effort felt like more of a success than the clothing drive insofar as the high school was not in Mississippi, but in the same town as the college, and it was easier to keep track of what was going on.

A month later, with the world still looking like an unjust place, Edgar and Mary started another program. On a brisk autumn Saturday while most of their fellow students were cheering for the blue and white at the football stadium, they paid a visit to a home for mentally impaired people. Before the sun set behind the polluted haze caused by the local steel mill, they had arranged a "Big Brother-Big Sister" program whereby students would spend a few hours a week giving friendship to those born into this world with brains and bodies of different bends. Edgar picked for his "Little Brother" a person named Dean who had the body of a thirty-year-old and the mind of one twenty-seven years younger. When Edgar introduced himself Dean was sitting on a beat up couch, drooling from both corners of his mouth while playing with himself under his weathered wool charcoal overcoat. He wore a red hunting cap under which his ears protruded like hairy old silver dollars.

Dean presented himself by saying three times that he was a boxer who had fought Joe Louis in New York City. When Edgar asked him when that was, he said it was about last week. When Edgar asked him where he had fought in New York City, he said "the same place we always do", then looked down and fingered a string of saliva heading toward a side coat pocket.

Mary established her relationship with a woman who was sitting in a corner clutching a purple purse and shout-talking angrily to herself. When Mary first approached her, she grabbed her purse more forcefully and bent towards the wall to protect it. Mary gently said everything was okay to which the woman responded with a growl and the sound "PLLLAH". Mary introduced herself, then asked her new "Little Sister" what her name was. She said "PLLLAH...PLLLAH" to which Mary said nice to meet you.

In order to recruit another twenty university students to befriend the other people in the home, Edgar decided to call on the members of the coolest male club on campus. He had acquaintances in the organization and he thought it might be a good thing for the coolest kids to see what it was like to be less than cool. He got plenty of volunteers. More than two dozen members immediately raised their hands when he asked who would help. He took their names and addresses, and within the week had them hooked up with their "Little Brothers" and "Little Sisters". They were supposed to go once a week for a minimum visit of forty-five minutes. When Edgar checked with the home a month later to see how things were going, the director said that besides Edgar and Mary, two other students had come, but each only one time. Two dozen had raised their hands and only two had gone. Edgar thought that if he was supposed to be among so-called Christians in a so-called Christian school, why wasn't Jesus wading around somewhere in their hearts? But evidently, He wasn't.

Edgar and Mary continued to see Dean and "PLLLAH" until the end of the school year. Dean still claimed to be a boxer, "PLLLAH" still clutched her purple purse, and Edgar and Mary were still Edgar and Mary.

After that fiasco, Edgar took on the war in Vietnam which was now in full demented bloom. His university, being a bastion of conservativism, was one of the few schools in America where the great majority of the students and faculty members supported the war. Naturally Edgar thought this extremely ironic: Jesus's children encouraging the use of bombs, bayonets, bullets, and napalm to kill people halfway around the world. But that was the way it was, so Edgar and Mary wrote a pamphlet. Actually, their pamphlet was a response to one the university President had handed out to the student body the week before. The President, a former U.S. senator, had said that all able-bodied men had an obligation to serve God and their country in the war in Southeast Asia. He didn't mince his words or leave open the door for any reflection on the part of the individual conscience. So Mary and Edgar got a few friends to chip in a few bucks each (they couldn't use freshman class student funds for such an individual project) and they printed their version of the story, i.e. Would Jesus have gone to Vietnam? Aren't we supposed to love our neighbours as we love ourselves? Mightn't it be possible that our "neighbours" stretch all the way to Vietnam? Does "Thou shalt not kill" mean anything at all? Mary and Edgar really just suggested that students think for themselves and make their own decision about a very serious matter. They didn't say "do this" or "do that" like the President had. But they almost got themselves thrown out of school for rocking the big boat. Within three days of the pamphlet's release, three thousand students had signed a petition for their expulsion from school. Fortunately, another three days later three thousand other students had signed a different petition supporting their right to say what they believed. The times were volatile, even in the conservative corners of citizenry.

Other than the pamphlet, they got hold of a documentary film on the My Lai massacre to show at the small campus theatre. Somebody's camera had picked up footage of Vietnamese women, children, and old people strewn about in a ditch with their bodies riddled with bullet holes, bullets shot from guns held by crazed U.S.

soldiers fighting a war against a form of government their leaders didn't agree with. The film was mostly pictures, but there was no doubt about what had happened. Some very innocent human beings had been dragged from their homes and slaughtered because they happened to be living in a place called North Vietnam.

The film was supposed to show four times, but it ended up being shown twenty-nine times. Edgar and Mary felt they were touching people somewhere. In any case, the war went on until it stopped. And when it stopped, all the dead were still dead and the deranged still deranged.

Edgar and Mary kept trying to save the world until the end of the school year. But little by little Edgar's enthusiasm waned. He began to think that if Almighty God and Son Jesus hadn't been able to do it, his chances were pretty slim.

So when the year finished Mary decided to transfer to Bryn Mawr outside of Philadelphia where she'd be with more people like herself. Edgar would stay put, but he would stop his campus activism and would spend the following year in the library reading books.

FOUR

EDGAR READS PHILOSOPHY AND RELIGION BOOKS AND THE TRUTH STARTS TO LOOK LESS TRUE

It was the comparative religion books that first got Edgar thinking. As he sat in a remote corner of the third floor of the school library where he hoped nobody would find him, Edgar realised that his church – Mormon – was one of many and that his religion – Christian – was also one of many and that all of the many churches and religions all claimed to be true. Edgar discovered that there were Gods and prophets galore, probably as many as there were fast food stores stuck to every artery around the campus: McDonald's, Wienerschnitzel, Kentucky Fried Chicken, Arctic Circle, Foster's Freeze, JB's Burgers, Burger King, Taco Bell, TacoTime, Orange Julius, and Jerry's Juiciest Burgers. These guys wanted our money and all the Gods and prophets wanted our souls. (Actually, thought Edgar, they, too, usually wanted our cash; they just never admitted it. In the case of Edgar's church, all members were politely asked to give 10% of their income to God, which meant to the church, which meant to the men in Salt Lake City who controlled the church. If they didn't give their dough (it was called "Pay a full tithe") it was also politely insinuated that Heaven might not be their post-Earth destination.

The more Edgar read about all the Gods and prophets, the more he thought he'd better start asking a few questions, questions like: "Does anybody really know what they're talking about?" or "Do people in other religions also get goosebumps which they interpret to be divine proof as to the truth of their beliefs?"

It wasn't long before the comparative religion books gave way to philosophy books. Edgar ploughed his way through "Introduction to Philosophy" to "Introduction to Epistemology" to "Introduction to Metaphysics" to "Introduction to Ethics". Then he started consuming platefuls of the big chefs themselves: Plato, Aristotle, Heraclitus, Spinoza, Leibniz, Kant, Hegel, Schopenhauer, Marx, Nietzsche, Camus, Sartre, and Merleau-Ponty. He even bit into a little Husserl and Heidegger. Edgar sat in that library from September to June trying to figure out what was true. The more he read, the less he thought anybody knew what they were talking about. The deeper he dug, the bigger the hole got. By spring the only guys he liked were the ones who gave no answers, like Nietzsche and Camus. The others sounded like his old Sunday School teachers, only they had bigger vocabularies.

FIVE

EDGAR'S CHURCH CALLS HIM TO BE A MISSIONARY AND HE
SAYS HE'LL GIVE IT A TRY

As his sophomore year ended, Edgar got a letter from the leaders of his church in Salt Lake City. He had been "called by God to be a missionary to spread the truth of the Gospel". They wanted him to go to France to help bring 60,000,000 lost French sheep into the fold. Edgar looked at the letter, typed on official church stationary and signed by the Prophet himself, as if it were written in Chinese. It stared at him. He stared at it. In between was a pocket of icy nothingness.

Like all good young men in good standing, he was supposed to "give" two years of his life to converting the unconverted. The church didn't know that Edgar's standing was in the mud. As a missionary he was supposed to tell people one basic thing: "I know that the Gospel is true." Edgar didn't know what knowing was, what the Gospel was, nor did he know what truth was. He did know that saying no to the letter was the equivalent of pitching darts at his family's good standing. His mother would cry, his father would wonder how the kid had missed the message, his sisters would think he had lost his noodle, and all the family's church-going friends would think the devil was doing dirty tricks on Edgar's otherwise agreeable mind.

Edgar looked at the letter again. This time his eyes saw the white of the page instead of the black ink. His brain roamed the spaces of nothingness, and for reasons unbeknown said, "Give it a shot. It can't hurt anybody. Learn some French. See Paris. Fake it for as long as possible." Then he thought, what the heck, maybe I'll even start believing it: Joseph Smith, founder, prophet, at fourteen doesn't know which church is true of the three or four in his New York town. Goes into a forest to pray. Angels and God or whoever show up to tell him none of the churches is true and he's supposed to start the true one when he's a little older. Gold plates will be given to him. On the plates will be the history of the New World from 2,000 BC to 400AD. Jesus came to America after his resurrection. Spread His word. It's all in The Book of Mormon. Seven million people now believe this story and go to church on Sunday and give their money and think they are right and that they will go to Heaven. Okay, I'll give it a try. Bye Mum. Bye Dad. Bye Jane and Julie. Pack your bags Edgar. Put on your white shirt and tie, your dark suit with your name tag stuck to the lapel, your most comfortable dress shoes, and you're ready to rumble. Learn those scriptures, memorise the right phrases, put a twinkle in your eye and a solemn grin on your dimpled face and say, "Yes, brothers and sisters, I know beyond a shadow of a doubt that the church is true, that Joseph Smith was – is – (we're timeless here) the prophet of God, that Jesus is the Christ (don't smirk at tautology!), and that only through living the Gospel can man enter the Kingdom of Heaven. Hey, why not? Sounds better than a lot of things. Get those French to stop drinking wine and smoking and drinking coffee and tea and fornicating with each other.

Edgar called his parents. They were pleased. They'd been waiting for the letter and the call. He'd begin his missionary training in a month. The path was straight and narrow. There was a light at the end. Onward Christian soldiers marching off to France with the Bible and Book of Mormon in hand to do what is right, right? Of course it's right if you believe it's right. Wrong. But who knows? Nobody. Certainly not me. Not me and this little pea brain I was given to make my way through this world of cinnamon rolls and garbanzo beans. Where's my passport? Put on clean socks and we're off. Salt Lake – New York, New York – Paris, Paris – Lyon by TGV. And we're in business folks. We're gonna spread the word of the Lord like peanut butter on warm baguettes. But first we have to train, practice, learn the scriptures. Eight weeks in monastic conditions. Thirty-five prayers a day. Pray when you wake up. Pray before breakfast. Pray before your first class. At the end of class. We ought to pray before we go to the toilet, but we don't. Pray before lunch. Pray after lunch. Pray that the prayer will we good. Pray for the faithful. Pray for the unfaithful. Pray before dinner. Pray before bed. Why, Edgar mused, don't we just say one big prayer for the whole universe? It would save time. But no, that's not the way the Lord works. Why? Is He deaf? He must get nine billion prayers a day. He must get tired of them, too. But no, that's not the way the Gospel functions. We keep praying to keep us faithful. To keep us in line. To keep reminding *us* of who we are, where we came from, and where we're going. To France, Brothers and Sisters. And then to Heaven. To the Kingdom of God. G – O – D. Where'd He get that name? Who cares? Plane is now boarding at Gate 12.

SIX

EDGAR FLIES TO FRANCE AND GETS HIT BY THUNDER

On the flight over Edgar knew things weren't going to be easy. First, he didn't know how long he could keep saying things he didn't really think were true. And second, there was the vow to never be alone with a woman for the two years he was to be a missionary. He was a late bloomer, but at twenty his juices were starting to warm up. The flight attendant who brought him his first apple juice on the flight out of New York bent down near his shoulder and smelled like the Garden of Eden. The plane jumped and she spilled a few drops on Edgar's pants. He smiled. As she smiled, the tip of her tongue was caught between her teeth in a fashion that made Edgar's belly feel like a washing machine. This narrow slice of moist pink flesh set on living white enamel, combined with her flowery scent, sent him into a spin. When she said "I'm so sorry" Edgar was only sorry she hadn't spilled more so that the whole process of wiping his pants in her presence would take longer. When she brought him a little towel her tongue tip was now fastened between her lips, lips that looked as if they had been gently waxed and inflated before take-off. Edgar had loved Mary in the sense of a working partnership, but here for life's first time, poor Edgar felt thunder behind the buttons of his white shirt. Why now of all times? Couldn't this stuff wait until he had finished his two years of spreading the Lord's message. It had to wait. Edgar had to turn off the machine. At least turn it down.

The attendant handed him the damp towel and he rubbed the damp spot on his pants which made a bigger damp spot. "It should dry fine," she said, to which Edgar said, "Yes, it should dry fine." She had a French accent. He had a virgin accent. The fellow missionary sitting next to Edgar said, "She's purty good lookin.'" He had a Texas accent. Then he said, "But we can' be foolin' wit nunna dem fillies fer a cuppa yirs."

"You're right," Edgar said.

"But it ain't gonbe easy," the Texas missionary said. "From what Ah hear, them French gurls is quick to the draw."

"Well, we know what we have to do," Edgar said trying to throw a little water on his fire. "We're doing the Lord's work."

"Raht. An ta do that we gotta keep ar hearts and mines as pure as Texas watta. Where yall from, anyway?"

"California. And you?"

"Galveston."

"There a lot of Mormons down there?"

"Ma parents urjanly come from Ahdaho. But yeah,

theys quite a few."

"Where you going in France?"

"It's called Dijon. It's where they make the mustard. How bout yussef?"

"Lyon."

"Whadathey make there?"

"I don't know."

"Ya feel ready?"

"For what?"

"The mishunery stuff."

"I guess as ready as I'll ever be. How bout you?"

"Ah ain't ready ad all. But Ah promized mu parents that Ah'd do it, so Ahma do it."

The same cabin crew member came back with another towel which she held in her thumb and forefinger with her pinkie floating alone above the rest of her hand in a delicate way Edgar had never seen before.

"I thought you might need this," she said with a smile that now hid her tongue.

I'm going to need a lot more than this, Edgar thought but didn't say as he looked past his shoulder and smelled her. He said, "Merci boekuu."

"From where do you come?" she said.

"From California," he said.

"And where are you going?" she said.

"To Lyon." he said.

"On holiday?" she said looking at his name tag.

"No, we're missionaries," he said looking at her name

tag that said "Air France".

"What kind of missionaries?" she said.

"Mormon," he said.

"Oh, I've heard of that before. Don't you have lots of wives and things like that?"

"Not anymore," he said and she smiled and walked up the aisle.

Dinner came and Edgar had another apple juice. This time the plane stayed still. A half hour later the trays were removed by the same hand with the same pinkie still floating under his nose like a flamingo feather. There was an announcement for the film and window passengers started pulling down the shades to darken the plane. Edgar lay back in his seat, snuggled his head into a deflated football-sized pillow, and closed his eyes. He fell asleep and fell deeper adream. He dreamt all the other passengers were sleeping and this angel in the Air France uniform tiptoed to his seat, slowly took his hand, led him to the back of the plane and down a curved flight of narrow stairs to the kitchen where stacks and stacks of snack trays were neatly arranged from floor to ceiling in two rows. They walked forward to a door which the angel didn't touch, but blew open with a breath of air that slid coolly and pianissimo past her partially-parted wetted lips. She looked back at him, clutched his hand a bit harder, then took a step. Together they flew into the thick milky dark.

SEVEN

"And you must be Elder Larsen," the man said.

"Nah," the Texan said. "Ah'm Elda Kane. Thizhere is Elda Lahsen."

"Hi," Edgar said, glad that the church referred to its missionaries by their last name rather than their first. Imagine, thought he, being called "Elder Edgar" all day.

Elder was the title all missionaries had based on their status in the Priesthood. You start out as a Deacon at age twelve. At fourteen you become a Teacher. At sixteen you jump to the status of Priest. Then your eighteenth birthday qualifies you for the status of Elder. Of course you have to be in "good standing" at every step of the way. Being in good standing means that you go to church most of the time, you don't drink beer with your non-churchgoing buddies in the parking lot behind the school, and you don't heavy pet with a girl – meaning you keep your hormonally infected paws off her three flowers. Interestingly, the rest of your behaviour and mindset doesn't seem to count much.

To be a missionary you have to be an Elder, so all the Elders call each other Elder. The man who greeted Edgar and Elder Kane had been an Elder, but wasn't an Elder anymore. He was the President.

"I'm President Wesley," he said, "your Mission President. And this is my wife Wanda. Welcome to France. Bienvenue en France."

"Thank you," Edgar said.

"And Elder Larsen, this is your companion Elder Britton."

"Hi," Edgar said to Elder Britton, a tall blond gangly young man with pimples and blue eyes. President Wesley was a grey-haired jovial-looking type in a dark blue suit, grey tie, and shiny black shoes. His wife looked older. She was plump, bubbly, clothed in a silver dress very similar to the kind Sister Marsing used to wear in Sunday School, and she had hair that seemed to Edgar to be tinted silver with a touch of blue. She looked proud to be who she was as did President Wesley. Elder Britton, on the other hand, looked like he didn't have a clue who he was. Without his name tag, "ELDER BRITTON – L'EGLISE DE JESUS CHRIST DES SAINTS DES DERNIERS JOURS" (Church of Jesus Christ of Latter-Day Saints), he would have passed for an over-dressed tourist lost in the Charles de Gaulle airport and in need of a good meal. President Wesley introduced another Elder, Elder Kendall, to the group. Elder Kendall was assigned to be Elder Kane's companion. All the Elders shook hands and said "Hi Elder. Nice to meet you Elder" until President Wesley's wife said, "How was the flight?"

"Longggg," said Elder Kane.

"Wonderful," said Edgar.

"Well, we'll get your bags and have a bite to eat, then get you on your trains to where you're going," President Wesley said. "Both of your trains are at about four this afternoon... What time is it now, Dear?... Eleven... So we'll have time to take you to the station." Though he didn't have to, President Wesley tried to meet all the new missionaries at the airport. He was their spiritual father away from home and he thought his initial presence got the young men off to a good start.

The group headed through the mob towards the baggage claim area. They looked rather like a family of penguins in their obligatory dark suits and white shirts. Edgar lagged behind a few steps looking left and right at clothes, faces, and signs that he had never seen before. He also hoped he might sneak a glimpse of the attendant toting a small black suitcase through the airport. He didn't see her, but by the time they got to the baggage claim, he felt he had seen just about every race, type, and colour of humanity in the universe. He saw Africans in long robes, Japanese tourists with cameras dangling from their necks, Indians and Pakistanis with their beautifully tinted brown skin, Arabs with turbans, to wit, more human types in ten minutes than he had seen in two years at the university. "France," he thought, "I'm in

France. There must be enough Gods here to fill up an encyclopedia. Islamic Gods, African tribal Gods, Hindu Gods, Buddhist Gods – many of them he had studied in the library back at school. All these people dancing to the rules of the Divine that they had been fed for breakfast through their youths, adolescences, mid-lives, and toward their graves. Some might change ships; some might stop believing altogether; some might be out to tell the world, like he was supposed to be doing, that their God was the One and Only, the True, the Real, the GOD." It all reminded Edgar of the Ricky Nelson song:

> You are the only one
> My one and only one
> Together we've had a lot of fun
> But what'll I do if you leave me

They picked up their bags and loaded people and possessions into President Wesley's Mercedes station wagon. While they drove into Paris, Elder Kane fell asleep. Elder Britton's nose started running and he kept wiping it with his hand. Elder Kendell and President Wesley talked about how many people had been baptised in the last month and the prospects for the next month. Sister Wesley and Edgar were on the right side of the car, she in front, he in back, and she asked him questions like where he was from, how many brothers and sisters he had, were his family members all active church members, did he leave a girlfriend back home, and was he glad he had been sent to France. Edgar answered them all, but had his eyes fixed on the boulevards and buildings that whizzed by him. They were big, they were beautiful, they were old. There were statues and trees and parks everywhere. There were bridges and the river. And the grey sky made everything look like it was attached to Heaven.

They parked at the Gare de Lyon and had lunch upstairs in the ornate Le Train Bleu with chandeliers and mural paintings all over the walls and waiters who were polite but barely looked at you. They all ate a "poulet à l'estragon" because President Wesley recommended it and, in any case, Elder Kane and Edgar couldn't understand what anything was anyway. They prayed before they ate. President Wesley asked Edgar to say it and he said:

Our Heavenly Father, thank You for allowing us to all be together here in Paris and for the safe trip over and for President Wesley and his wife who picked us up at the airport and for the Prophet and the church authorities and bless them that they might lead the church as You wish and bless this food that it might nourish and strengthen our bodies and do us the good we need and we say these things in the name of Jesus Christ. Amen.

At three-thirty they went down to the quais to their respective trains. Elders Kane and Kendall were to board the TGV to Dijon on platform 7. Elders Edgar Larsen and Dennis Britton were to be packed into car 117 on platform 12 on the TGV to Lyon. President Wesley said he'd be down to see them all soon. He said a short prayer before they boarded thanking the Lord for their safe trips and blessing them that they would do the work of the Lord as best they knew how.

They boarded. Whistles blew and they were off.

EIGHT

In the mouth of an LDS Church person the word "investigator" stands for someone who is interested, maybe, in being baptised a member. It has nothing to do with "investigating" crime or other such societal nuisances, but only with the possible entry of a new soul into the Kingdom of God. In the mouth of a missionary, an investigator is a potential person to lower into the waters of baptism, and, in so doing, adding another point to your scorecard. Of course, no missionary or mission president wants to admit he or she is keeping score. But if the goal is to bring people into the fold, the more people that are brought in, the better one appears to be doing one's job. Or so it might seem.

Edgar had no interest in baptising anybody because he had no idea what he might be baptising them into – God's holy realm? A business? A social group with a religious name? Nothing? Elder Britton, his constant companion, had been a missionary for a year and had baptised one person. Whenever an investigator showed real interest, he got as excited as a boy on his second date.

So when Edgar met old Madame Jeanne Lachat at the market one day and she seemed to take an interest in the church, Elder Britton was overjoyed. He and Edgar had been ringing doorbells, walking the streets, and casting their rods to the waters of Lyon for nearly a month since Edgar arrived and had had nary a nibble. Here was a woman – probably about seventy-five and not far from death's red carpet – whom Elder Britton saw to be genuinely interested in the true church of God. Edgar saw a sad disappointed creature who had probably lost faith in Catholicism and was looking for another way to spend her Sundays other than in front of the television set. Naturally Edgar never told Elder Britton or anybody else this, but that's the way he felt.

It was Madame Jeanne Lachat who had approached Edgar as he was choosing an apple from a box at a stand at the outdoor marketplace on the island between the two rivers, the Saône and the Rhône. He couldn't decide between a Gala or a Golden. She had noticed Edgar's fine face, i.e. his loose wandering hazel eyes, his soft cheeks, his dimples when he smiled, his straight nose, the curve of his upper lip, and his slightly wavy brown hair. Simply put, Edgar reminded Madame Jeanne Lachat of a boyfriend she had had fifty-five years ago. She wondered if Edgar was her ex's grandson or something.

"Bonjour," she had said staring at Edgar's face.

"Bonjour," Edgar had said.

"Are you any relation to Jacques Beauchamp?"

"Not that I know of."

"You look just like him. He was my boyfriend."

"When was that?"

"Fifty-five years ago."

"Oh."

"You look just like him."

"Really. I'm flattered, madame."

"Can you sing?"

"Not very well."

"He could sing. He used to sing Le Temps de Cerises to me while we walked right here along this river in the spring."

"That must have been beautiful," Edgar said meaning it.

"It was more than beautiful. It was Heaven itself."

"I'll bet it was."

"It was. Until he married someone else."

"Oh, I'm sorry."

"He went into the army. I wrote him letters. I prayed that he wouldn't get killed. He didn't get killed. I did. When the war was over he came back to Lyon and married a girl from Belgium. The last time I saw him he was getting on a train for Brussels. He said he'd be back. As far as I know he never came back. I haven't seen him for over fifty years."

"You must have really loved him."

"I did. You look so much like him, I thought maybe you were one of his grandchildren or something."

"No, madame. I'm American. I'm a missionary."

"Who do you preach for?"

"The Church of Jesus Christ of Latter-Day Saints."

"Never heard of it."

"You're not the only one."

"What do you believe in?"

"Oh, we're Christian and all that. We just have other books besides the Bible that we consider holy scripture."

"Really. What books? Things like Madame Bovary or Le Rouge et le Noir?

"No, but that's an idea. No, we have The Book of Mormon and The Doctrine and Covenants."

"Never heard of them," the woman said shaking her head and trying to focus on Edgar's nose at the same time.

At this point Elder Britton, who had been patiently listening and wiping mucous from his nose, stepped in. "If you'd like to know more about the Gospel we can come and visit you sometime."

"The Gospel? Who are you?" Jeanne Lachat had had her eyes fixed on Edgar all the time and hadn't noticed the tall young man next to him. "You don't look like you're related to Jacques Beauchamp. You look more like a Charles Trenet."

"I'm Elder Britton. I'm Elder Larsen's companion?"

"Are you gay?"

"No. We're missionaries. Who's Charles Trenet?" Elder Britton asked.

"A singer."

"You must like music?"

"I do. I listen to Charles Trenet and Edith Piaf."

"So if you'd like to know more about our Gospel, we can come and visit you."

Jeanne Lachat gave the Elders her address. They seemed harmless, most of her friends were dead, and she still could appreciate the sound of a human voice. She lived on the Rue de Condé not far from where they were standing. They could come by the next morning at ten. She would make them coffee. No, they didn't drink coffee. Then she would make them tea. No, they didn't drink tea. Then she would make them hot chocolate. That would be fine. They said goodbye and the Elders watched Madame Lachat waddle off through the crowd holding plastic bags filled with leeks, onions, potatoes, and more leeks.

"Nice woman," Edgar said.

"She really seems interested," Elder Britton said.

"In what?"

"In the church, Elder... what do you think?"

"Well, you could have said music."

"Elder Larsen," Elder Britton said taking on a serious air, "sometimes I think you need to pray a little more for the Spirit of the Holy Ghost to be with you. I mean sometimes I think you don't fully concentrate on the missionary work."

"You're right, Elder," Edgar said. "I do sometimes

forget why I'm here. It's good I've got you for a companion. You're the best companion a missionary could have. You keep me focused on the Gospel." Elder Britton smiled as Edgar spoke. The fact is, Edgar was serious insofar as Elder Britton was the perfect companion in that he basically left Edgar to his thoughts, he wasn't pushy, and he only asked Edgar to pray together with him five or six times a day. Some senior companions had their new junior companions on their knees before the Lord every half an hour or so.

Edgar also loved Elder Britton because he was who he was and obviously couldn't have been anybody else. Edgar felt this way about everybody. This is one of the reasons he didn't believe in the teachings of his church. He didn't see Madame Jeanne Lachat as an "investigator"; he saw her as a lonely old woman who saw a young man who reminded her of her unforgettable old boyfriend and who invited them to her house because she liked them and had nothing else to do. That she – of all people in Lyon – was interested in the church was purely based on a set of unique circumstances and not on anybody's righteousness or unrighteousness. The problem for Edgar was that the church taught that only people who accepted the Gospel could go to Heaven. Edgar saw that accepting the Gospel had to do with freak circumstances and nothing else. How could this be the dividing line between Heaven and less than Heaven? How would God keep his door closed to the other million and a half people in Lyon just because they happened to be Catholic or Muslim and didn't have an old boyfriend who looked like Edgar? Elder Britton was a Mormon because he was born one, born and raised in Ogden, Utah. Had he been born in China he'd be a Communist or a pro-Tibetan underground Buddhist. What Edgar couldn't take was righteousness taking credit for its own righteousness and thinking all the other poor souls were unrighteous because of their own unrighteousness. Ah, the bells of freedom toll when we want them to. They ring-a-ding-ding when they make us look good to ourselves, and hence to God.

Edgar chose the Gala apple, the redder of the two, small, but firm and smooth to the fingers. It cost a franc. He didn't eat it right away, but shined it, held it, turned it, then put it in his side coat pocket.

He had arrived in September. It was now October and the buildings along the Rhone were catching the sun and were changing colour as if suddenly being painted by the invisible hand of a magical morning god.

NINE

The first time the two missionaries climbed the three dark flights of stairs to Jeanne Lachat's apartment at 24 Rue de la Condé, they wondered how the old woman did it every day with her grocery bags. By their fifth visit they stopped wondering; it was normal.

On arriving in France, Edgar was immediately struck by how few fat people there were. Now, after two months, he knew why: people walked and they climbed stairs. Home in America people drove their cars to the supermarket, then parked in their garage which was usually attached to the kitchen. In Lyon they walked to the marketplace and from shop to shop to get what they needed almost every day. Then they walked up a few flights of stairs. Then they took the garbage down those flights of stairs and walked back up.

Madame Lachat gave the young men hot chocolate on each visit. She added cookies on the third visit. On the fifth she prepared lunch of leek soup and gâteau au fromage. She didn't drink wine in their presence anymore, and she was glad she didn't have to get up at the end of the meal to make coffee.

She had now heard the whole story of Joseph Smith praying about which was the true church, the angels, the gold plates, the Urum and Thummun (the special glasses Joseph wore to translate the plates), the Book of Mormon, the pioneers, Brigham Young, the Word of Wisdom (the rules about eating and drinking), the Celestial Kingdom (the penthouse where you lived with God as opposed to Terrestrial and Telestrial Kingdoms, Heaven's version of a Motel 6 where you resided if you were too obtuse or too stupid to accept the Gospel), baptism of the dead, and baptism of yourself. Elder Britton had done most of the talking because he spoke better French and because he believed what he was saying. Edgar threw in a few sidelight remarks about eternal life with no beginning and no end, but other than that he watched Elder Britton work when he was not distracted by the potpourri of old objects crowding Madame Lachat's two room apartment: the portrait of de Gaulle behind the sewing machine on the ancient table next to the beaten velvet moss-green sofa, the white birdcage inside which lived a fake parrot, the line of orange, green, and burgundy cushions on the sofa, the shoe container that hung in the hall on the wall which was covered with tired gold-framed prints of reproductions from the Louvre, the radio console in the corner next to the electric heater, the stacks of Paris

Match magazines next to and behind the TV, and the cross with Jesus drooping sadly alone on the wall behind the vast tattered leather armchair in which Madame Lachat always sat. Madame Lachat, like ninety-five percent of the French, had been raised a Catholic. After thirty years of Mass at the Eglise de Sainte-Croix just down the street, she suddenly stopped going. She decided that the Pope should live in France, not in Italy, and given that he didn't, he was a phony in all his creamy robes and gold wallpapered mansions and all. She liked the Mormon idea of the unpaid clergy and the simple suit-and-tie dress. She also liked Elder Larsen. After the fifth lesson Elder Britton could feel she was filled with the Spirit of the Holy Ghost and was going to accept the Gospel and be baptised. He was right. As they were having chocolate mousse (the missionaries' favourite treat) for dessert after the sixth lesson and lunch, Jeanne said she had prayed the night before and was ready to be baptised. She had no family other than a brother in Marseilles, so nobody was around to be mad at her for changing religions. And as she looked at it, she wasn't changing religions because Mormons were still Christians. She was only changing pilots.

Elder Britton set the baptismal date for the twenty-second of November. He told Madame Lachat she would have to be dressed in white and explained the process of baptism by immersion, i.e. you go completely under water. Madame Lachat said she couldn't swim, to which

Elder Britton responded by assuring her that he would be holding on to her and that she had nothing to worry about because the font was never more than four feet deep. He called President Wesley who said he was thrilled and that he and Sister Wesley would come down from Paris for the occasion. Elder Britton then politely asked Edgar if he wanted to baptise Madame Lachat given that he was the one who discovered her. Edgar said that it was she who had discovered him and through no merit of his own, so he'd be more than happy to let Elder Britton have the honour. Edgar's generosity made Elder Britton's mouth beam like a horizontal flame. He would double his number of converts. He would have something to write home about other than the weather and the truth of the Gospel. Of course Edgar was in no way being generous because he had no desire to baptise anybody. He was a missionary whose mission was to be pleasant to those around him and to try to decide what he was going do with the religious education he had been given and in which he was presently immersed twenty-four hours a day.

At nine o'clock on the morning of the twenty-second of November Elder Britton and Edgar were eating apple tarts on the street outside their favourite boulangerie next to the Place Bellecour. Elder Britton's nose was running and Edgar kept watching to see if a trail of mucous would make it onto a bite of the pastry.

"Elder, you'd better watch that runny nose," Edgar offered before it was too late.

"Oh, thanks Elder. Even though I know it's not colder than in Utah, it sure seems colder here. Must be the humidity."

"Must be."

"They sure don't make tarts like this back home."

"They sure don't."

"I wonder why."

"I don't know Elder. The Lord works in mysterious ways."

"Do you think the Lord has anything to do with how people make apple tarts?"

"If I could answer that question, Elder, I'd be the smartest man on Earth."

"Well, what do you think?"

"Do you really want to know?"

"Sure I do, Elder Larsen."

"I don't have the slightest idea about where and on what the Lord lays a helping hand."

"You don't?"

"I can't imagine He would favour anybody or anything over anybody or anything else."

"Well don't you think He helps Madame Lachat find us – or rather helped us find her?"

"So what about the other million people in Lyon?"

"I guess they're just not ready for the Gospel yet?"

"Okay Elder, your guess is as good as any. What time

is the baptism?"

"At two o'clock. I told Madame Lachat we'd be by to get her at twelve-thirty."

"What do you want to do until then?"

"Let's look for investigators."

"Okay, Elder."

So they walked across the bridge to the other side of the Saône and up to the old town. They tried to talk to anybody who would listen. The only person who said "hello" back was a beggar. When Elder Britton tried to explain that they were Mormon missionaries, the man said, "God is dead, fortunately."

At twelve they ate a sandwich in a little café next to Madame Lachat's apartment. At twelve-thirty they rang her doorbell. She answered dressed in what looked like the wedding gown she never got to wear.

"Nice dress," Edgar said smiling.

"It was my mother's. She gave it to me. Unfortunately, I never got to wear it. At least I can still get into it. She was a little chubby and I would have had to take it in. Now it's just right."

"Well, what a good idea to wear it today for this special occasion," Elder Britton said.

"Do you have something to change into after the ceremony?" Edgar asked.

"Oh, no..." the old woman hesitated. I forgot about that."

"You'll be all wet," Edgar said.

"Yes. Let me get some things."

They took the bus to the chapel which was in an area called Les Brotteaux. President Wesley and his wife were waiting for them just inside the door. At two, Elder Britton and Madame Lachat walked down the tile steps into the blue water of Lyon's only LDS baptismal font. He walked backwards holding both her hands. Elder Britton blessed her in the name of the Father, the Son, and the Holy Ghost, then he threw her backwards and under making a large splash. He half slipped and fell into the water up to his neck. She came up gasping for air, but by the time they got out of the pool she had a smile on her face. She shook herself like a wet dog, then went back to the dressing room to change her clothes.

TEN

EDGAR HAS A TALK WITH THE PRESIDENT

After the ceremony President Wesley told Edgar he thought it would be a good idea if they had a little talk. Edgar said that would be fine. Sister Wesley had brought a cake for the post-baptismal celebration, so she, Sister Lachat, and Elder Britton went into the foyer of the chapel to eat. President Wesley took Edgar into a small office room with blue chairs and a picture of Jesus alone on the wall.

"Elder," the President began, "Elder Britton tells me you're a fine companion, but that you're not a hundred per cent into your task of spreading the Gospel." He looked deeply into Edgar's eyes. Edgar looked at his mouth and wondered if there was a ventriloquist behind him.

"You're right," he said, seeing no reason to be less than frank.

"What is it that holds you back? I know you come from a fine church home and that you've had a wonderful Gospel upbringing."

"I have. But that has nothing to do with how I feel. My family is one thing and I'm another."

"Why do you say that?"

"President Wesley," Edgar said sliding his tongue behind his lower lip, "if the only reason a missionary is a missionary is because he comes from a good Mormon family, then something's wrong. That would mean that a good Catholic should be a good Catholic because his good parents were good Catholics. We could say the same thing for Buddhists and Seventh Day Adventists and Communists. If we're just a repeat of our parents, I wouldn't say that's much of a compliment."

"But if your parents live the true Gospel of the Lord Jesus Christ, then certainly you want to also live that same true Gospel?" The President's glance was meant to be inspired by none other than God. He saw himself as a mouthpiece of divinity.

"I love my parents, but I don't know if they know or anybody else knows the truth about God or a Gospel or whatever."

"Elder Larsen, have you fasted and prayed about your testimony?"

"Of course. We pray all the time. But I have no idea who we're praying to. It usually sounds like we're praying to try to make ourselves feel good and righteous. People pray in every religion and they think they're getting answers and inspiration from their own God. Why should we be any different?"

"Because, Elder, ours is the true God."

"But all churches say that."

President Wesley had had one other missionary like Edgar a couple years back. Maybe not so lost, but suffering from the same doubts. He had got on his knees with the young man and prayed that the Lord might fill the Elder's doubting heart with a knowledge that the Gospel was true. When he had finished his prayer, he and the young man had both had tears in their eyes and the stray lamb was back in the fold. He suggested he and Edgar do the same. Edgar said fine. As they knelt on the azure carpet President Wesley set his eyes on the picture of Jesus, took a profound gulp of air, then slowly lowed his eyelids and said his prayer:

Our Father in Heaven, we are on our knees before You today to ask that You help Your dear son, Elder Larsen, Elder...Elder...Edward Larsen, to look deeply into his heart and to know that the Gospel of the Church of Jesus Christ of Latter Day Saints is the one truth in this world, that Joseph Smith was – and is – a true prophet and that Jesus is the Christ and that we missionaries are doing Your glorious work. Bless Your son Elder Larsen that his faith will become as pure and clear as the crystal waters of ... of ... of a baptismal font. And we say these things in the name of Jesus Christ. Amen.

They rose to their feet and President Wesley looked into Edgar's eyes. They were as dry as two marbles in a desert. For that matter, the President had not been moved to tears either. He put a hand on Edgar's shoulder and said, "Elder, stick with it. Keep giving it a try. I'm sure the longer you're here on your mission, the more profound will your testimony grow. Elder Britton is a fine missionary and together you will do the Lord's work as He wants you to."

Edgar didn't say anything but gave his shoulder a slight hitch and the hand slowly pulled away.

"I must go back to Paris now, but I'll be in touch with you soon."

"Thank you, President Wesley," Edgar said, now quite certain this would be the last time he would see the man. He wasn't sure when or how he would stop his mission, but he knew he would very soon.

ELEVEN

Edgar had about a thousand dollars. And his father had given him an American Express credit card in case of an emergency. He could live for a while.

Missionary rules were such that he was constantly with his companion, except to go to the toilet or take a shower. Elder Britton always knew where he was. He'd have to leave in the middle of the night, wait for the first morning train to Paris, and hope it left Lyon before Elder Britton woke up and found that he was gone.

They normally were out of bed by five-thirty and saying their first morning prayer over a bowl of cornflakes and a cup of hot chocolate. Edgar woke without an alarm at four. The world was black and he couldn't lighten it up without jeopardising his departure. He tiptoed out of bed and dressed in the clothes he had left on the chair next to the desk. Elder Britton slept soundly a few feet away. His suitcase was under his bed. He got on his knees and slowly pulled it out. Since all his clothes were essentially the same – dark suits, white shirts, dark ties and socks, and his special religious underwear – it didn't really matter if he didn't get everything. He grabbed a few things out of his two drawers, then stealthily walked to the bathroom and fingered the glass shelf above the basin for whatever he could grab without making a ruckus. He closed the suitcase, went into the hall, put on his overcoat, and was out the door.

Lyon hardly breathed at four o'clock in the morning. There was barely a sign of a human soul until he saw a silhouette in the light of the window of the boulangerie at the Place Bellecour. A soft twisting fog dangled beneath the streetlights. His suitcase wasn't heavy and he walked quickly along the Quai du Docteur Gailleton next to the Rhône. The water looked like a sheet of tar with a few horizontal strips of tinsel. In two months he had come to love the rivers and the thought that they continually flowed towards the sea.

He had a ten-minute walk to the station. He put his hand in his inside jacket pocket to be sure his passport and wallet were there. He turned up the Rue de Condé and as he passed Madame Lachat's entrance, he kissed his hand and blew the embrace off the inside of his fingers. He hurried through the empty Place Carnot and into the main hall of the station. There was a crumpled string of winos strewn across the benches in the waiting room. Edgar found the list of departing trains on the wall next to the kiosk that was not yet open for business. The first train to Paris was at 5h47. He should be okay. Elder Britton would not rise until five-thirty and it would take him a few minutes to realise Edgar was not there. If he did run to the station, Edgar would be gone.

And he was, almost alone in the front car where he had taken refuge as soon as the doors of the train had opened at five-thirty-five. Now they were chug-rolling over the river and out of Lyon. Edgar sat up high in his seat looking out, but mostly seeing his own reflection in the black window. He had had to go. After his talk with President Wesley he knew his world was not theirs. The people had been fine, but he couldn't go on playing the part of one who was supposed to be sure that this hunk of a spinning world had been poured, moulded, sculpted, directed, and loved by a God and was not just some cockamamie cosmological accident – or whatever. Edgar didn't know one way or the other. But he couldn't take sides. He couldn't say, "I know...." He couldn't bear his testimony to anybody. The only testimony he had was that the planet was full of believers who believed in multifarious deities and multifarious notions of good and truth. What he could do, however, was to steal out of the missionary apartment, out of the missionary world, and into Paris, a city – like all cities – of life, death, passion, pleasure, food, excrement, work, crime, loyalty, treachery, goodness, and sin, all blended together under grey, blue, or black skies. He could go and, for a while anyway, live the life of Edgar, not the life that he had been born into. He had read about Camus's Paris, Sartre's Paris, and a little about Henry Miller's Paris. In three hours he would discover Edgar's Paris.

There were only a few other people in the compartment with him. From where he sat he could see only one, a man across from him of about fifty dressed casually in brown corduroy trousers and a black turtleneck sweater. Their glances met once and the man smiled at Edgar and partially nodded as if to say, "We know each other from somewhere, don't we?" But they didn't speak then and the man spent most of his time reading a paperback book in English of what appeared to be short stories called "Too Far to Go".

Edgar would have liked to change his clothes, but he had nothing in his suitcase any different from the missionary outfit he had on. He looked down and noticed he still had his name tag on. Discreetly, he reached across his chest, unpinned it, and dropped it in the metal garbage container under the fold-out table next to the window. He thought of Elder Britton which made him think of his parents. Surely they would soon be informed about his disappearance. He would send them a telegram saying not to worry and that he was fine. He was twenty years old and though he loved all he had lived at home, he needed to peer into a few new windows of the world. He didn't want to hurt anybody, but they had to understand: to be somebody you've got to at least try to do it your own way.

The train pulled into the Gare de Lyon at nine o'clock. He took his suitcase off the rack above his seat and walked to the door. As he waited for the train to stop the man in the black turtleneck said in English, "Are you American?"

"Yes. How did you know?"

"It's not too hard to tell. First time in Paris?"

"More or less."

"Enjoy yourself. It's my favourite city."

They got off and the man disappeared into the river of passengers lugging themselves and their belongings along the quai towards the exits that released them to the city. Edgar was glad that the man hadn't asked any more questions. He didn't know what he would have said.

TWELVE

Paris can be friend or foe to the American visitor. Much usually depends on the predisposition and attitude of the guest. Does he try to speak the language? Does he seek out the new or does he want "America" on foreign soil? Does he bitch about the food and the price of a Coke? When he asks for directions, is he polite and does he begin with a humble "Excusez-moi" or does he approach the Parisian with the ugly American "Hey, can't somebody around here tell me...?" Does he complain about the weather, the traffic, the metro smells, and the crowds, or does he set his eyes on a civilisation made to pluck the finest strands of the human sensibilities?

Edgar was the perfect guest. His French was cute and passable. He wanted to be nowhere else. He had a respect for the writers he had read who had breathed on the city's boulevards, bridges, and balconies and who had perished in its cafés, hospitals, and corroded corners. He didn't want his past; he wanted to discover a new world. So when he walked down the quai, straight out of the station and past the taxi stand, he smelled the air and saw the creamy grey buildings with their open white shutters and iron balustrades and it all gave him goosebumps, goosebumps like the ones he used to get in church as a kid when the congregation threw their voices into that last burning refrain.

He crossed the street and walked up the tree-lined pavement of the Rue de Lyon past restaurants, small shops, banks, porno theatres, and hotels. His eyes and heart bounced like pinballs ringing up a string of bonus points in a hot machine. Of course he didn't know where he was headed because he didn't know Paris. But the best visitor is one who doesn't know where he is going and doesn't really care. He walks and sees the lines, forms, and colours around him like a painter in another painter's studio. He smells the city like a lover breathes in his beloved's groin.

Until he gets thirsty, that is, and he slips into a café past the Place de la Bastille on the Rue St. Antoine and orders his life's first beer. The "Une bière, s'il vous plait" slips out of his mouth like a fish out of a wet hand when the barman approaches him. He has not thought a thought; he has simply seen a wet beer in a hand of the man next to him at the counter and so he has asked for one, too. The Kronenbourg comes bubbling with a soft white cap that Edgar smears on his lips as he sips his first drops of the heretofore forbidden syrup. It feels better than it tastes. But it is the first and is simply opening the door for the many others that will come with what the world calls "an acquired taste". Though Edgar doesn't quite finish it, he has drunk enough such that after he pays the barman, picks up his suitcase, and walks back into the street, he will feel a sensation that he has never before felt in his twenty years on Earth: the world will be moving under him and around him and his head will be unweighted. He will smile and will trot on under the thick motherly canopy that is the Parisian sky. He will meet a moment where Heaven is the earth.

Edgar keeps walking up the Rue St. Antoine until it becomes the Rue de Rivoli and a flood of shoppers oozing in and out of department stores. He comes to the openness of the Chatelet and goes left to see the fountain. He sits on its ridge and gazes at the stairwell with the circled "M" over it that is sucking in and releasing streams of rapid walkers. He then gets up and crosses the street onto the Quai de I. Mégisserie. He senses that the Seine is just across to his left, but he stays on the right pavement. It gets narrow because it suddenly becomes a row of plant and flower stores that display their goods outdoors. These soon give way to animal shops, almost as if, thinks Edgar, he were walking backwards through Plato's hierarchy of being: plants to animals to man and to God. On the pavement in crowded cages there are chickens, geese, and rabbits waiting for life or death depending on their buyers' intentions. Inside the shops there are dogs, cats, hamsters, and mice that can most likely count on a more extended longevity.

The pavement gets less crowded and Edgar sees in front of him the walls and gardens of what he will soon know is the Louvre. He ambles right and then onto a gravel path that leads him into the enclosure of mammoth buildings that kings and queens built to allow themselves to live like kings and queens. He sits down on some steps near a young man with a backpack, a thick Peruvian sweater, hair to his shoulders, and eyes cooled with a few deep inhalations of a marijuana cigarette. The young man sees Edgar with his short hair, creased slacks, polished shoes, and overcoat.

"How's it goin'?"

Edgar's comes back with a soft "Hi."

"You speak English or anything?" hums the hippie.

"Yes," Edgar answers.

"Where ya from?"

"America."

"I figured that Jack. Where in the land of the free?"

"California."

"Oh yeah. What part?"

"The Bay Area."

"No shit? Me too. What city?"

"Pleasant Hill."

"I'll be damned. I'm from Walnut Creek. Ya look like ya just got outta the fuckin' army?... So how long ya been in Paris?"

"Maybe an hour."

"No shit! And ya came straight to the Louvre?"

"The Louvre?"

"Well where the hell ya think ya are...? At Fisherman's Wharf?"

"It's my first time here and I just walked from the train station."

"Ya walked from the fuckin' train stain to here? Which station?"

"The Gare de Lyon, I think?

"Ya walked halfway cross Paris. Well, this is it – Big Daddy Louvre." The hippie opens his arms like bird wings, then closes them and stares at Edgar. "Hey man, really...Do ya always dress like that?"

"No. Only lately."

"Are ya a travelin' salesman or summin'?"

"Not exactly."

"Well where ya stayin'?"

"I don't know. Like I said, I just got here. Do you know any nice cheap places?"

"As a matter of fact, I do. When I got off the train this chick gave me this address and it's cool. A youth hostel not far from here on the Jean-Jacques Rousseau Street. I been there for three days and I'm leavin' tomorra. I'm in a room with two other dudes and actually I think they're splittin' today, so hell, you could probably stay wid me."

"How much is it?"

"In dollars or fuckin' francs?"

"Francs is fine."

"Fifty a night. That's about ten bucks."

"Sounds good."

"Listen, I gotta go over there now. Why don't ya jus' come on wid me and check it out."

They rise in unison and the hippie guides Edgar two blocks to the youth hostel. The girl at the desk is pleasant and accommodating and puts Edgar in the third-floor room with his only friend in Paris. The two roommates have in fact split, so Edgar and his friend each have a bunk bed to himself. The room has a sink and is quiet and clean, except for the hippie's pile of junk at the foot of his bed. The shower and toilet are down the hall. The hippie must have used them first because surprisingly neither he nor the room stinks. Edgar throws his suitcase on the top bed, takes off his coat and shoes and lays down.

"Ya gunna bag some Z's?" the hippie says.

"Just a few, maybe," Edgar says.

"Check ya later, man. The key's on the table. My name's Luther."

"I'm Edgar," Edgar says. Luther makes a fist which means both power to the people and nice to meet you.

"Hey, uh, if ya need ta borrow any of my clothes or anything, feel free," Luther says.

"I'm fine," Edgar says.

THIRTEEN

EDGAR GOES TO THE LOUVRE AND GETS HIGH

When Edgar woke up, for a moment he didn't know where he was. His nap had been the sleep of a dead man, deep and black and hermetic. He rolled over in the sagging bed and saw the hippie's pile of junk. His mind put one and one together and the room made sense anew. He got up, threw some water on his face, dried with the thin towel the girl downstairs had given him, and sat back down on his bed. For the first time since he had left Lyon, he thought of Elder Britton and what must be going on in the mission headquarters: phone calls to his parents and – maybe – the Lyon police, President Wesley wondering what he should have noticed about Edgar and what he should have said to him the day before, a search for a new companion for Elder Britton, and bundles of prayers by all the Mormons who knew that the missionary had disappeared. *Our Father in Heaven, please protect Edgar and bless him that he is okay and out of harm's way.*

And he was.

He changed his clothes replacing his white shirt and suit coat with the only sweater he had, a chocolate brown V-neck that his mother had knitted for him in case France got really cold. It had never left his suitcase. He might shop tomorrow. Today he would visit the Louvre.

He went downstairs and the girl at the desk looked up from the book she was reading, smiled, and said "Au revoir". She appeared to be about his age with auburn hair that was pulled on top of her head and fastened with barrettes giving her the look of a happy rooster. Her nose was slightly pugged and Edgar noticed her cute chin.

"Au revoir," he said. "Je vais au Louvre."

"Amusez-vous," she said.

The Rue Jean-Jacques Rousseau was only about three hundred yards long. Rather short for a guy who wrote so much, Edgar thought. It was primarily restaurants and bars. It ran into the Rue Saint-Honoré which Edgar crossed and soon found himself back where he had met Luther. He migrated towards the herd of people around the entrance to the museum.

When you walk into the Louvre for the first time, what happens usually depends on you: how you think, how you feel, your sensitivities, your inklings about the past and the present, your notions about form and colour and creation, whether or not you're hungry, bored, itchy, in good company, happy, sad, alone, dying, living. Most people buy their ticket, go in, wander around, eventually follow the signs to the Mona Lisa or the Venus de Milo, then leave. They have been to the Louvre.

But for a rare few, the Louvre is something else. It is a place where one's own life gets put on hold for a while and the spirit gets thrown into a whirlpool of blood, brain, beauty, and the human condition. Young Edgar wasn't necessarily this deeply sensitive soul, but he was a changed man when he walked out. He spent three hours ambling at a snail's pace thinking not so much about the individual works in front of him, but about the fact that somebody – some human person – was behind each of the pieces he saw. Each painting and sculpture had a maker who had a life, a set of beliefs, hopes, fears, visions, and a death. Edgar felt the vastness, but at the same time he sensed a closeness, a strange shared humanity, a sense that, like it or not, we are all in this together.

"Where ya been?" Luther asked when Edgar came in the room. "I thought ya fell off the Eiffel Tower or summin'." He was stretched out on his bed smoking what Edgar assumed was a joint.

"At the Louvre. Quite a place."

"Yeah, I checked it out the other day. But I like Beaubourg better. It's got newer shit."

"Where did you go, Luther?"

"To see Jim Morrison... my main man. He buried here in Paris. Went to his grave. People all over the place, sittin' around with candles and shit." Luther chuckled and said. "I see ya didn't borrow none a my clothes."

"No, I'm okay. But I might do some shopping tomorrow."

"Hey man, ya like to get high?" Luther said extending the smelly joint in Edgar's direction.

"Actually I've never tried it."

"You never smoked a fuckin' joint and yuz how old? Ya in a sect or summin...?"

"Well sort of, but it just hasn't been part of my lifestyle. I come from kind of a conservative family."

"Well, hey, ya in Paris now. Join the real world. Wanna try it man?"

"Sure, why not," Edgar said, "I had my first beer a couple hours ago."

"Ya only live once, man. It good shit. I got it in Lyon."

"You've been in Lyon? Me too." Edgar took a rather deep puff and coughed.

"Try again," Luther said. "That's normal for a rookie." Edgar did and after a couple more drags, started to get talkative.

"Actually. I'm a Mormon," he said. "Well, sort of. I was. In fact, I was a missionary in Lyon until this morning."

"All I know bout Mormons is they got a shitload of wives... That ain't a bad idea..."

"They used to have lots of wives. But that went out a long time ago."

"Sorry to hear that... I mighta joined my damn self."

"I just didn't believe it anymore, so I decided to leave." Edgar was semi-stoned and didn't mind telling his story. He went through family, the mission training, Elder Britton, and even Madame Lachat. This morning seemed like months ago. He took another puff and said, "So now you understand my clothes."

"Ya man," Luther said. "Ya got some guts takin' off like that."

"No, not really," Edgar said. "It would have been a lot harder to stay. I just did what I had to do."

"Well, hey, whataya doin' tonight? I'm leavin' tomorrow ya know, so lez do summin."

"Sure," Edgar said, "How about us getting something to eat. I'm pretty hungry"

"Good place to start."

Luther got up and opened the window to air out the room. They both put on their coats, and, like brother and brother, clopped down the worn wooden stairs to the street.

FOURTEEN

As they were standing at the corner waiting for the light to turn green to cross over to the Pont-Neuf, Luther looked up, down, then at Edgar and said, "Sure ya don' wanna borrow any threads? Might help ya land a fox?"

"A fox...?"

"A chick."

"A chick...?"

"A woman man... Don't tell me you ain't never been down no rabbit hole?"

Edgar finally understood what Luther was talking about, but no, he hadn't been down a rabbit hole. As a matter of fact, he had hardly been up there. Being a Mormon, he had missed out on that part of the Sixties revolution, too. But now, he thought, before answering Luther, he really had nothing holding him back. "Like I said," he said, "it just wasn't part of my culture either."

"Well, Eddie, we got ya some pot. Now we just gotta find ya some pussy. You'll be in the heaven ya been preachin' about, but ya won't have to die first."

"How about if we eat first, if that's okay," Edgar said.

"Cool, Eddie. Man can't live on pot and pussy alone. Let's get one a them them Keebob sandwiches they got over in the Latin Quarter."

"Sounds good."

Luther was the official tour guide as they drifted across the Pont-Neuf. It was getting near six and dark as Edgar's eyes clicked onto the sky behind the Eiffel Tower. It was losing its last swabs of grey. The air above the Seine was unusually still and when Edgar looked down at the river, it was as black and flat as a Bible. Luther noticed that Edgar was having a little trouble walking so he slowed the pace. He was basically always high, but he had forgotten what a first timer like Edgar might be going through. They walked along the Quai des G. Augustins where the used book sellers were closing up shop, then went across the Boulevard St. Michel and into the bonanza of international restaurants. They found a Kebab outlet next to the Huchette Theatre and had two sandwiches each.

"Good shit, huh Eddie?" Luther said as he swiped his tongue across his teeth trying to release the cornered bits of lamb.

"Yeah, they're very good." Edgar lifted the collar of his charcoal overcoat. "It's a little chilly standing here. What do you want to do now?"

"Paris is Paris, baby. We can go anywhere. But let's get summin to drink in a café first. You can tell me the rest of your life story."

Kathy and Sarah had had the same idea first, so when Luther and Edgar sat down at the table next to them, they were already into their second glass of white wine. Luther went right to work.

"You two muss be American," he said the first time he got eye contact.

"How'd you guess?" the blonde blue-eyed Kathy-from-Kansas-State answered.

"Divine intervention," said Luther. "Or I got some kinda extrasexual perception or summin."

"I think you mean 'sensual'," Kathy-from-Kansas-State said. "Extrasensual perception."

"Actually, I think yuh both mean 'sensory'. Extrasensory perception," said Sarah-from-Savannah with a lovely Southern drawl.

"Gawdam," said Luther. "You must be an English major from Georgia."

"And you must be not as dumb as you look," said Sarah-from-Savannah making it sound like "An yooo muzz not be azz duhm azz yooo look."

"Thanks. Nicest thing I've heard since I've been in France. So where you two from?"

"I'm from Georgia. Savannah, Georga." Her accent had Edgar memorised.

"And where you from?" Luther said to the blonde blue-eyed Kathy-from-Kansas-State.

"Kansas. I go to Kansas State."

"You two sistas?" Luther said flashing a thin smile.

"Very funny," said Sarah-from-Savannah. "We met in the train from Venice and we've been travellin' together ever since. So what's with your friend over there? Can't he talk?"

"I'm Edgar," Edgar said.

"So you can talk. And what's King Kong's name," Kathy-from-Kansas State said gesturing to Luther.

"Luther," Edgar said. "We're both from California.

"Ya all brothers "

"How'd ya guess?" said Luther.

The waiter finally came and Luther ordered a pastis. Edgar didn't know what to order, so he ordered a pastis, too, not knowing what it was. The girls ordered another glass of wine. The boys were cute enough to hang around a little longer.

"Ya ever had a pastis?" Luther asked Edgar.

"No."

"You'll love it. Liquid licorice. A couple of em'll fuck you up. Make you feel like you was back in Berkeley."

"You from Berkeley? Sarah-from-Savannah said.

"Not too far from there," Edgar said. He's from Walnut Creek. I'm from Pleasant Hill."

"Never heard of 'em," said Kathy-from-Kansas-State.

"We met today at the Louvre."

"We were there, too. Did ya like it?"

Edgar felt Luther tap his leg under the table. Edgar had no idea Luther was trying to transmit a message to the effect that if they stuck with the conversation and were cool enough, they might have a chance to score. Edgar had never really played this game. To Luther's slight disapproval he said, "Yeah, I thought it was wonderful. I spent about three hours just wandering around."

"We didn't even get to see the Mona Lisa," Kathy-from-Kansas-State said. "There were all these Japanese tourists in front of it. And they wouldn't leave. But otherwise it was all right."

"It's too big," Sarah-from-Savannah said." "What did you think, Kong?"

"Luther, honey," Luther said with his sexiest smile. "But I kinda like King Kong! Actually, I went a couple days ago. I like Beaubourg better."

"Where's that?"

"It's over by Les Halles. Looks like a damn Pac boat. It's got the modern stuff."

The four of them drank and talked for another half an hour. Edgar needed lots of water to get through the pastis. But it actually did taste like liquorice and wasn't bad. Luther invited the girls to come over to the youth hostel for a drink or to smoke a joint or something. They said they had to go back to their hotel first. Luther explained where the hostel was and said they'd be downstairs in the lobby at ten. The girls said they'd come.

They didn't. At ten-thirty Luther went outside and smoked another joint. Edgar went upstairs to bed. He had wanted to say goodnight to the girl at the reception desk, but she wasn't there. An older man was in her chair reading a newspaper. Edgar brushed his teeth, fell on the bed, and was asleep before he could get his pants off.

FIFTEEN

EDGAR SENDS A TELEGRAM TO HIS PARENTS AND MEETS
SOUTINE

The next morning Edgar awoke to the sight of Luther
stuffing his stuff into his backpack. Edgar rubbed his eyes
and remembered that his only friend in Paris was
leaving. "Well, I'm outta here," Luther said closing the
last pocket on his pack. Edgar got up, thanked Luther for
everything and told him how nice it was to have met him.
Luther said, "No shit man. It's been a pleasure. Be cool."
They quickly exchanged home addresses, but Edgar
knew they probably wouldn't have much in common if
they were back in California. Luther tried one last time
to give Edgar a pair of beat-up jeans, but Edgar kindly
refused. He refused a joint, too. They shook hands.
Luther said he was going to Amsterdam, flashed the two-
finger peace sign, and out the door he went.

Edgar sat on his bed, bent forward because of the
upper bunk, lowered his head, and rubbed his brow. For
a second he almost wanted to cry as one does when one
senses that one's supports have suddenly fallen away. But
he quickly decided he was happy to be where he was. He

also reckoned that if he had found Luther so quickly, he'd find other contacts as well. Then he thought after the couple of months of constant companionship of Elder Britton, maybe a little solitude wouldn't be such a bad thing.

He thought, however, that he should contact his parents before their worries blew out of proportion. They didn't deserve to suffer. He had only been gone a day but, depending on when the mission authorities had contacted them, they would have had time to get worked up. He would send a telegram instead of calling. That way, there would be no discussion. Dear Mom and Dad, As you must now know, I left mission. I'm fine. Just couldn't go on. Need time alone. Don't worry. Love to all, Edgar. He'd be brief and to the point and he would send a more complete letter later.

He put on his charcoal overcoat and went downstairs. The girl was at the desk tied to the telephone. Today her hair was down and she wore a spinach-green button-up sweater that was not buttoned at the top three buttons. This simple sight of her skin above the crooked "V" of her open sweater was enough to twist the imaginary screw that went from Edgar's head to heart with a southward detour. He waited and discreetly watched until she was off the phone.

"Can I help you?"

If you only knew, thought Edgar. "Yes," said Edgar.

"What is it?"

I've been a Mormon missionary for the past six months which means I've been unable to touch or smell a woman in order to guarantee my purity, but now I've stopped the mission and my purity is now the way I feel about you, meaning, as Luther would say, you turn me on, thought Edgar. "Do you know where I can send a telegram?" said Edgar.

"Sure. About two blocks away on the Rue du Louvre. Number 52, I think."

If you say one more word I'm going to jump over this counter and kiss you, thought Edgar. "Thanks," said Edgar.

"You're welcome."

I don't know what's happening to me. Is it that I'm just horny or is it that there is something in the way this French girl moves, talks, dresses, and smiles that drives me crazy? thought Edgar. "Au revoir," said Edgar. And out the door and down the three steps he went heading left on the narrow pavement.

He sent the telegram as planned and as soon as it ticked towards America, he somehow felt a weight or a halo had been lifted from atop his head. It was now official. Edgar had said goodbye or at least had made public the fact that he didn't believe that the religion he had been born into was true. How often this must happen, he thought as he walked out into the street. But when it happens, what happens? Obviously a person can't stop being who they are overnight. But who are they? For more than two years Edgar had already deeply questioned his Mormon heritage. This wasn't a one day to the next thing. Even as a kid, Edgar had asked questions that Sister Marsing and his other teachers couldn't answer. What I'm doing, he thought, is merely an extension of who I am. It is not a radical step. It is a step with the same foot in a different shoe. I was told that the meaning of the world was one thing. That I don't believe anymore. With what shall I replace it? Need I replace it? Mormonism was an all-encompassing proposition. It explained everything. It explained God, man, sin, redemption, Heaven, Hell, good, bad, the reason man was on the earth. He was on the earth to earn a spot at God's side in Heaven later on. That was it. That was all. That was his purpose. But if this is not true, if this God is not real, what is the purpose?

Edgar's thoughts were not banal. They were his and they were very close to him. It was as if he had been a user of a language and he had decided to stop using the alphabet that built that language's words. What do I make of the world now? How do I interpret it and give it sense, meaning, light and dark and shadows? The alphabet was the material and the mind was the glue. Now there would be new material and the mind would again glue things together.

Edgar went across the street and wandered west up the Rue Saint Honoré toward the Jardin des Tuileries. There was sun today which seemed to give Paris a different feel and smell. He went into the park and sat in a chair next to the pond below the Musée de l'Orangerie.

New material? he thought. There is still the same world. Whether I believe the Christian-Mormon story or not, this world is still here. I'm still here. The park, the fountain, the people, Paris, the Eiffel Tower, the Seine, the ocean, the land and sky... I can believe whatever the hell I want to believe, but I still must deal with this world. I still must either sit in this chair, get up from this chair, break this chair, or wipe it clean when I leave. No matter what alphabet I have, I have a world.

Edgar stayed in that green chair for about an hour. The morning sun, his thoughts, and the passersby were pleasant enough to keep him there. He finally got up and walked towards the small museum at the corner of the park. He had no idea what was inside. The sign said "Orangerie." Maybe it's a museum about oranges, he thought as he bought his ticket.

It was the opposite of the Louvre: quaint, cosy, uncrowded, well-lit and small. It housed paintings, not oranges. (Though there was an orange on a table painted by a man named Cézanne.) Edgar walked around looking at the names of the paintings and the painters, and then the pictures themselves. Cézanne, Utrillo, Matisse, Renoir, Rousseau, Modigliani, and the big Monets downstairs. But it was the three Soutine paintings that he looked at the longest. Especially the slab of meat. This man (Edgar assumed Soutine was a man) had painted a hanging slab of meat with reds, blues, yellows, blacks, whites, and purples. Here, thought Edgar, was a new alphabet. A slab of meat in a museum in Paris. And next to the slab of meat, an old poor skinny woman in red. And next to her an ugly little baker with a wrinkled baker's hat. But the baker wasn't ugly and the woman wasn't poor and old and the meat wasn't just meat. As he stood there, Edgar felt like if there was such a thing as Christianity today, this was it. This painter Soutine was giving value and respect to all life. All life was divine. All life had value. There were no winners or losers. Or else the losers were the winners. The last really first. The old woman was the queen. The little baker the king. The meat divine.

Edgar went outside. Soutine came with him. Together they went around La Place de la Concorde, up the Champs-Elysées, and down a side street where Edgar ate a cheese sandwich. Before he ate it, he looked at it: half a baguette, butter, Camembert cheese. It looked back at him: twenty-year-old, pimples gone, cute enough face, walnut eyes, behind those eyes neither a Mormon nor a hippie, neither a man nor a boy, neither a follower nor a leader, neither a saint nor a thief... just a twenty-year-old in Paris wondering what to do.

SIXTEEN

In Pleasant Hill, Edgar's home town of about twenty thousand people, you either drove or rode your bike if you wanted to go somewhere. In 1974, when he left for France, there were essentially no buses or other form of public transportation. Hitchhiking was a possibility, but stories of dangerous characters – on both sides of the seat – were making it less attractive. Until he turned sixteen, Edgar's mother had been his principal source of movement. Their house was tucked in a hill two miles from the nearest school or commerce, so walking anywhere wasn't on the daily menu. "Thanks Mom," he'd say when she dropped him and a buddy or two off at the bowling alley, the golf course, the movie theatre, or the baseball field. "You're welcome, Edgar. Have fun," was always her answer.

Walking back down the Champs Elysées after his sandwich, Edgar figured he had probably already walked at least three miles that day. In Lyon, he and Elder Britton must have walked four or five miles a day trying to find somebody – anybody – who would listen to their

(Elder Britton's) story about the purported truth of their vision of the cosmos, according to which God had let man squirm around for many a century until he finally called on Joseph Smith to clean up the mess. Few French would listen, so on and on they had walked. In America, Edgar really had only walked on the golf course, and that was because he never had enough money to rent a cart. But France had taught him not just to walk, but to enjoy it. He had also learned to look around while he walked to see things you don't see in a car. After a mere twenty-four hours in Paris, Edgar felt that he had a deeper relation with this city than with, say, an Oakland or a San Francisco, which he had visited hundreds of times, but always in a motor vehicle. There, he knew the freeways. Here, he thought, I know the pavements. And in a car you get to know the smell of the car; on foot you get to know the smell of the city.

Edgar sat down in a café on the Champs-Elysées with a view of the pavement fully aware that his drink would be expensive, but, not being in a hurry, he considered he was merely paying rent for his chair for an hour or so. After he sat there for a while he decided his twenty franc Coca-Cola was cheaper than a cinema ticket and watching the human parade in front of him was as good as most movies.

When he finally got up at about two o'clock, his legs were tired. He saw the Metro sign at what he didn't know was the F. D. Roosevelt station. He went down the stairs without a clue as to what he was doing. Would he be able to get off near the hostel? Did he need the right change? Would it be "dangerous", like in New York City, to venture underground, especially alone? What if he got lost?

When he approached the swinging entrance doors, he got his first whiff of the Parisian Metro. It hit him as hard (if not harder) as the first whiff he was soon to get when he would come face to face with the moist labia majora that grew like an orchid out the crotch of the girl at the hostel desk. When he went through that door at the Champs-Elysées F. D. Roosevelt station, the Paris subway instantly became a part of him. The odour jumped through his nostrils and went to a permanent resting place in his head. In future years, every time he would get into the Metro he would feel like he was back home, like he had returned to the gigantic motherly matrix, the labyrinthine womb that had received him that second day in Paris, and that that was where he was supposed to be. Was it the smell from the tyres, the brakes, the walls, the human bodies? He didn't know exactly what the odour was. But it was the Paris Metro and, like the labial flower, he loved it. It took him in when he was tired and delivered him, whole and happy, to another beautiful part of the city.

In this case (he had quickly figured out the system), it released him at the Louvre-Rivoli stop. When he mounted the stairs and saw the buildings and sky and recognised where he was, he sensed the little thrill one can get when one knows, temporarily, where one is.

SEVENTEEN

When he walked in the hostel she was at the desk and Edgar, in his joy, spontaneously spoke to her. He said hello and he told her of his walk, of Soutine, of the Champs-Elysées, of the Metro. He asked her what else he should visit and she told him the Marais quarter where she lived. He asked her if she would be his guide and she said she'd be glad to be. He asked when and she said she was off tomorrow. He said where can we meet and she said she was preparing for her exams and needed to work in the morning so how about at the Chatelet fountain at two. He said fine, I know where it is. She said have you been to the Pompidou Centre and he said no, but I've heard about it and would like to go. How about the Picasso Museum she said and he said the same thing though he didn't know it was there. What are you studying he said and she said French and Art History and he asked if she liked it. Most of the time she said wearing another button-up sweater this time the colour of a drying leaf that wasn't buttoned all the way up and the V made Edgar's head half cough and his stomach do a back flip. When she talked she sounded like a love song so he asked her now what she planned to do when she finished school and she said she had two more years left and that she hadn't really given it much thought because she had really just wanted to live in Paris. He said where are you from and she said Les Rousses in the Jura mountains near the Swiss border and where are you from. America he said and when she said where he said California and when she said what part he said near San Francisco, near Walnut Creek, in a place called Pleasant Hill. She smiled big and said believe it or not I've heard of Walnut Creek because when I was studying English in high school I read a book about Levi Strauss inventing jeans in 1850 or thereabouts in a place called Walnut Creek. I didn't even know that said Edgar and then two backpackers came in smelling like greased metal so Edgar said goodbye see you tomorrow and went up to his room.

Tomorrow at two came slowly but it came and Edgar was at the fountain before she was and while he was waiting he realised he didn't know her name. He had left the hostel at one and had walked along the Seine, eaten a crêpe au sucre, and had retraced his steps on the pavement between the animals and plants on the Quai de I. Mégisserie. He sat on the edge of the fountain and wondered what her name might be. He explored the alphabet: Anne, Abigail, Alice, Arabella, Brigitte, Bernadette, Bonnie, Betty, Clara, Clair, Christine, Cindy, Celine, Catherine, Charlotte, Camille, Doris, Debora,

Daisy, Elizabeth, Ester, Eileen, Florence, Fanny, Fiona, Frances, Francine, Grace, Gail, Gloria, Ginger, Heather, Helen, Heloïse, Isabelle, Iris, Jane, Julie, Jennifer, Janet, Jennie, Jessica, couldn't think of a K then came up with Kirsten or Kristen and Katherine, Lucy, Linda, Laura, Lulu, Lucille, Lila, Lili, Lucinda, Monica, Mary, Marlene, Mable, Martha, Missy, Marcia, Nathalie, Nadia, Nadine, Nora, Odile, Olivia, Patty, Pam, Penelope, Priscilla, couldn't think of a Q, except Queen which wasn't really a name except for being the name of his grandfather's horse, Rose, Rosemary, Rita, Rebecca, Rhonda, Sally, Susie, Sandra, Sarah, Suzanne, Samantha, Sherilee, Terrie, Tina, Tamara, Teresa, Ursella, Violet, Valentine, Vanessa, Victoria, Wendy, Wanda, couldn't think of an X, Yolanda, Zelda. As Edgar thought, some of the names were attached to faces and others weren't. His sisters, Jane and Julie, were in there, his mother Ester, his grandmother Isabelle, his first girlfriend at age five, Odile Fleisher, Rhonda Trout, the girl who followed him around for two years in junior high, but otherwise the names were sounds that meant "female" to him, sounds that dotted his past like California poppies in a summer field.

It was chilly sitting at the fountain, but with the sights, noises, and smells of Paris, Edgar didn't mind the wait. She came, a couple minutes after two, in a long tan coat that rose above reddish-brown boots like a fan. Have you been waiting long she said leaning forward to kiss

Edgar's rising cheek. No he said lying but really not because it had not seemed so. You know I just realised sitting here he said that I don't know your name. Patricia she said which hadn't exactly been on his list. I'm Edgar he said thinking that her perfumed cheek had smelled like sweet cinnamon. She took his arm under the elbow and said let's go to Beaubourg first. She told him the Pompidou Centre was also called Beaubourg and was named after the president George who like all presidents wanted to leave a legacy.

On the escalator up towards the painting collection Edgar looked down on the square below and at the yellowy cream buildings around it and felt as if he were rising with an angel because she was. These things happen. She showed him Matisse first and then Kandinsky and Klee and then Mondrian Marc Miro Léger Pollock Picasso and Francis. She said these were her favourites and told him that as far as she could understand modern painting generally took the object out and left only the colour because that is what the eye really sees. Only lines and colour. He said it was the first time he had really looked at pictures like this but he saw what she meant and then she said for example when you look at me I'm really just a two-dimensional surface of lines and colours like a photograph. I only become three-dimensional when you experience me but this is in the meeting of your other senses and your mind and not in your eyes. For your eyes the world is always flat she said.

They finished with the pictures and went upstairs to the café and had a drink. She asked him why he had short hair when the style was long and why his clothes were mostly white shirts and a dressy overcoat. They spoke French. Because I was a missionary and that was the way we had to look and dress which was all right with me. It was the rest which wasn't all right meaning having to say I know this is true and everything else isn't when for me I have no idea what truth is. Then he thought of Simon and Garfunkel who said the only truth I know is you and he thought how she looked like a great painter made her because her face was proportioned like a kitten's and he looked at her over the rim of his glass of Coca-Cola and he shivered a little. How long were you a missionary she said and he said if you count the training programme almost six months. He said I left Lyon only a couple of days ago but it seems much longer. I noticed you she said because basically all I see from America are hippies all dressed the same who can't speak a word of French and who say like ya know and ya know like all the time even when they're asking for a room. Ya know like how much is it like for a room. That kind of thing. You didn't talk that way she said. I didn't quite see the relationship between you and your friend which made me wonder. Wonder about what he said. What you were doing together she said. I had walked from the train station to the Louvre and met him there. He was nice enough to help me out. He's gone you know he said.

They walked through the Marais and she showed him where she lived by pointing a finger up a building to about the fourth floor where the window was open a crack. Then they went to the Picasso Museum and this time she didn't say much but watched him watch the paintings which were moving insofar as they basically didn't stop walking a slow walk all through the building because he was fascinated with each picture and kept wanting to see the next. He loves women Edgar thought thinking that if he would paint and draw so many he had to love them. She only said that he recently died and that many consider him the greatest force in painting in the twentieth century. Edgar said he is lucky he was a painter because he's not as dead as he otherwise would be because his pictures live on. She looked at his face.

He didn't go up to her room that day or night because she knew it would be a little fast, but the next night they had dinner together at a little five-table wood dark restaurant on the Rue Vieille-du-Temple and drank wine and she invited him up for dessert which was chocolate mousse. Her room was about the size of his father's car with a bathroom and kitchen tacked on for good measure. There was a bed, a radio, a rug, an electric heater, a poster, a cupboard, a bookcase, a small table, and a chair. There was another chair in the kitchen which she brought out with two bowls and spoons and the chocolate mousse. She told him it was her grandma's recipe and she told him about her grandma who got her education on a farm but who was smarter than most people she met at the university. She told me to love the grass that the cows eat and the cows that the men eat and the men who love the grass and the cows. The rest are all half-baked she said she said. He fell more in love with each verse of her song.

So what happened was that they kissed and rolled clothed and fell asleep on the bed with the electric heater on and woke up at about four and she reached at all his buttons and zippers and helped him peel it all off and then she crossed her hands at her waist and with a simple upward pull pulled off her sweater and they were naked on the covers when he started kissing her everywhere and she him and he came to the labia majora damp with desire's dew and he tongued it gently up and down and side to side until he edged on to her and they joined. When they finished he licked around his lips and smelled his fingers and fell asleep with his nose in her neck and hair.

Edgar was one of the lucky ones: his first walk in Eden's Garden was real and reciprocal and so right that guilt had no way to butt in and mess things up.

EIGHTEEN

What Edgar didn't know at the time was that these moments don't come by too often. Not the kissing and the copulation and other acts physical, but the real union. Of course the world is plastered with acts physical between A and B, otherwise there wouldn't be so many of us. But rare are the comings together where A and B want nothing but each other, where there is no thought of something missing or askew, where the blend of body and brain and blood is so complete that neither A nor B feels for a second that there could be a C.

These moments can last an hour, a day, months, even years. But they are "moments". Edgar would find this out later. He would learn that in order for a "moment" like he had that night with Patricia Tinguely to be possible, a great number of conditions must be present and must come together at the same time. A scientist might say, "like what it takes for life to occur in the universe." Just their meeting was miraculous in itself: HE – called to France for his mission, decides to leave on day X, decides to go to Paris, walks from the Gare de Lyon, by chance ends up at the Louvre, meets Luther, Luther takes him to hostel, etc., etc...; SHE – only one in her family to go to university, chooses Paris, knows her father is strapped for money, finds job where she can read and study during slow moments, almost hired by hotel in Pigalle, ends up at hostel, etc., etc.... And then there is the emotional side: HE – never too taken in by his church's teachings about the evils of the flesh, once he thought God might be just a much-used word corresponding to either nothing or an unknown, his already weak notion of sin got watered down even more leaving him open to such a meeting, Patricia had something other girls he had known didn't have, i.e. she seemed self-contained and not trying to be somebody else and he felt she felt her body to be as natural and ephemeral as a cotton cloud, he had left a world and was so happy to find another one, she gave off light and an odour that charmed him, her voice was music to his ears; in short, for the first time in his life he was intoxicated by the simple presence of a woman; SHE – had split with her boyfriend a month before and he, she decided, had been something of an imitation, she had felt he was not interested in her, but in showing her to his friends, when she saw Edgar she saw something out of the ordinary and he was polite and not pushy and his French was adorable, she sensed that Edgar was open to the world like her grandmother had taught her to appreciate, she sensed he wasn't out to shoot off his wad, but was in love with her, she liked the curl of his lips, she liked the way his eyes saw from his own heart and not the world's heart.

All this made their night in her room perfection. A man and a woman from different continents and different cultures took the threads of their pasts into that bed on the fourth floor in the Marais and wound themselves together into one winged wondrous spool.

These moments happen, like the first single-celled organism, if ever there was such a thing.

NINETEEN

EDGAR DISCOVERS THE FRENCH BREAKFAST

When Edgar woke up that morning the tiny room smelled like a pot of coffee. It was a quarter to eleven when he rolled over towards the window and saw Patricia laying her lone little table with spoons, knives, bowls, butter, jam, and the baguette she had already been out for. She was wearing a black T-shirt that said "Golf de Mont St. Jean" and a pair of beige jeans. His mouth was cottoned sticky when he opened it to say "Bonjour".

"Are you hungry?" she said coming to the bed to kiss his cheek.

"Smells good," he said. "You know I've never had coffee before. It was against my religion."

"Well, it's part of mine," she said. "Morning without coffee is like night without day."

Edgar put on his socks, pants, and shirt and slid into the chair closest to the bed.

"Do you want to try it?" she said.

"My nose already has. It's good."

She brought the coffee pot and a pitcher of warm milk

from the kitchen. She poured some of each in the bowl in front of him.

"I thought the bowl was for Cornflakes," he said.

"This is France, Edgar," she said pronouncing it "EdgAAARR". Do you want sugar?"

"How do you do it?"

"One clump in the morning."

"Well, when in Paris do as the Parisians do."

She cut the baguette in half, then cut her half in half, then cut the half half longways. He did the same. She buttered and jammed two of the half halves and so did he. They ate and drank the coffee that dissolved the cotton in his mouth.

"It's really good," he said. "The coffee."

"Fifty million Frenchmen and the rest of the world can't be all wrong," she said. "Was it really against your religion?"

"So were a lot of other things I've tasted lately." His tongue and lower lip licked the ledge above his upper lip, though she didn't notice it.

"I was raised a Catholic, but on our farm the Pope didn't have any more status than Bruno the bull," she said.

"Do you play golf?" he said re-reading the emblem on her T-shirt.

"No. My father turned the farm into a golf course a few years ago because none on my brothers wanted to spend his life milking cows."

"How many brothers do you have?"

"Four. And two sisters. My father didn't fool around. Well, actually he did fool around – still does, I think – but he paid enough attention to my mother to make seven of us. My brothers all work on the golf course. One of my sisters does, too. She runs the little hotel and restaurant. My other sister is married and works in a factory across the border in Switzerland."

"And you're the only one to have gone to the university?"

"Yeah. Being the last, my mother used to read to me a lot at night. I think she was just tired and was looking for an excuse to sit down. Anyway, she read me enough stories to fill two brains before I started school. I haven't stopped since. Reading myself, that is. So when I finished the required school, I said 'I'll go to Paris and read some more.' And here I am. I loved the farm and the golf course is all right, but I wanted to come to Paris because I had read so much about it."

"Does your family ever come?"

"No time to. I go home for Christmas. It's only a five-hour train ride. Do you want some more coffee."

"Sure. The bread is delicious."

"Not better than your cornflakes and pancakes?

"How do you know about pancakes?"

"Like I said, I read a lot."

"I'm starting to convert," he said smiling. "Your butter tastes like it just came from the cow."

"How did you know butter comes from a cow? Most Americans don't know that."

"My grandfather came from a farm, too."

"Lucky you."

Edgar looked at Patricia and sensed he was looking at himself had he been a female. This breakfast tied to the heels of the night he had just lived had plopped him, thought he, square under the apple tree in Eden's Garden. So they shared the apple to the last slice and when finished, rubbed bellies again and locked. As the stone straight snake headed the bottom of the hole, they sang hallelujah together and carved a new chapter of Biblical lore.

TWENTY

Patricia had to go to work at three that afternoon, so Edgar decided to go shopping.

"Just go down the Rue de Rivoli," Patricia had said. "There's more junk there than you could fit on the moon. You'll find everything you need."

Edgar decided he would first replace his underwear. As an Elder and a missionary he had been required to wear a special single piece – top and bottom together – underclothes that were supposed to protect you from harm's danger or danger's harm or sin's suggestion or suggested sin or whatever you needed to be protected from. Interestingly, thought Edgar as he entered his first department store, Patricia had said nothing about his undergarments when she had helped him remove them the night before. That morning he hadn't put them back on.

All he could find in the way of briefs were the tight bikini affairs that the French were noted for. The loose boxer-style underpants that he and his friends had favoured in high school were nowhere to be found. The boxer shorts would make their way to continental Europe ten years down the road, but in 1975 Edgar had to settle for a three-pack of skimpy, ostensibly sexy, genitalia-hugging, thigh-squeezing underwear for the special price of 39 francs. Edgar also found a pair of jeans, so when he left the store he could be seen clothed anew below the waist and pulling with doubly-bent fingers at his upper legs trying to stretch the elastic band that he felt was gently strangling his none-too-big unaccustomed thighs.

As he walked up the pavement he realised he needed T-shirts as well. A few metres ahead was an outdoor stand where a visibly cold young man was selling postcards, miniature Eiffel Towers, and sweatshirts and T-shirts with Parisian reminders silkscreened across the chest area. The man, rocking from leg to leg with fisted hands at his sides, accosted Edgar when he hesitated in front of the stand. Edgar responded and for seventy francs bargained his way to a navy blue "University of Paris" sweatshirt and two white T-shirts unsparingly decorated with Alexandre Gustave Eiffel's architectural wonder. He figured when he got home his sisters would want the T-shirts for nightgowns.

He had what he needed; his coat, shoes, and white shirts were fine. Fashion wasn't at the forefront of Edgar's thinking. But a gift for Patricia was. Do you give somebody something after one day? Why not? Edgar thought, thinking that in the end the real pleasure was for himself. Giving, he had learned in his university days, usually did far more for the giver than the receiver. But what to give to his newly beloved? Surrounded by "more junk than you could fit on the moon", what piece would show what he wanted to show, or what piece would at least give her a hint of pleasure? He hadn't a clue. He had never been here before. He had never walked down a pavement knowing that in a few hours he would see the woman who had accompanied him to the grassy plot in Eden's Garden and who was now irrevocably injected into his brain. I'll just walk, he thought, and if something comes it comes. I'm in no hurry. She isn't expecting anything.

When he got to the Hôtel de Ville he went across the plaza toward the Seine and continued over a bridge to what he didn't know was the Ile St. Louis. The street down the middle looked like it was made in Hollywood or Disneyland except for two or three semi-smashed piles of dog doo on the narrow pavement. The buildings and signs attested to the glory of French architecture. Halfway down the street was a food store specialising in cheeses, cut meats, and wine. The French like food. Patricia is French. My first present will be for her mouth. The man inside was red-cheeked and pleasant and when Edgar explained he was looking for a small gift, the man suggested a slice of foie gras. Edgar had never heard of foie gras and even after the man explained it to him he still didn't get it. But the light pinkish beige colour reminded him of Patricia's skin so he got some. The man cut an inch slice, wrapped it in waxed paper, scotch-taped the sides, and put it in a plastic bag.

Edgar walked back to the hostel along the Seine. He buried his hands in his coat pockets leaving the bag to swing from his wrist like an idiot pendulum. His crotch was tight, but that didn't keep his eyes from sucking in the grey-tinted greens, yellows, whites, and browns of Paris in the light of late November.

TWENTY-ONE

She kissed him across the counter when he gave her the sack with the foie gras at the hostel. He told her to thank the red-cheeked man in the shop.

"You've got a new roommate," Patricia said. "Everything was full, so I had to put him in with you. He's from Chicago. I think that's what his passport said. He seemed nice and he didn't stink. I told him he'd be in the same room with a preacher from California."

"You didn't?"

"I didn't. I think he's upstairs now."

"I'll go up and try on one of my new T-shirts." She blew him a kiss.

When Edgar opened the door, his new roommate was shaving in front of the mirror. "Hi. I'm Russ," the man said with a half-closed mouth to keep the shaving cream from dripping off the area above his upper lip.

"I'm Edgar. Nice to meet you. Where are you from."

"Chicago originally, but more recently from New Mexico. I'm going to school there." He looked more like a teacher than a student, so when he saw Edgar's look of wonder he added, "I'd been assistant coach for the basketball team for ten years and I had had enough so I decided to go back and do another degree. What about yourself?"

"I'm ah... I'm in Paris to see Paris, I guess." The man Russ ran the razor down the sides of his face. He wasn't pushy so Edgar said, "Actually I was a missionary in Lyon and I decided to stop, so I came here."

"What kind of a missionary?"

"Mormon, or – if you prefer – the Church of Jesus Christ of Latter Day Saints."

"We had a couple Mormon ballplayers at New Mexico State. Nice kids. Never caused any problems. At least we knew they weren't getting high before games. So why'd you stop?" He had finished shaving and was towelling his face.

"I didn't believe in it, so I couldn't preach it anymore. It's as simple as that."

"Sounds fair to me. That's kind of what happened to me and basketball. I just couldn't put my heart and soul into what's really just a dumb little game. I mean it's a great game and all, but it gets so blown out of proportion these days. The money, the cheating, the hype. It's really a circus. Hey, but life is what you do while you're waiting to die, so I guess people have to do something to fill up their time. I just decided to take a different road, at least for a while anyway."

"So what are you studying now?" Edgar asked noticing that his new roommate had left a small garden of whiskers at the bottom of his chin.

"Writing. Literature. I came to Paris to try to get a little inspiration for a story or two. Actually I came to Paris because my girlfriend and I just split up and I figured a change of scenery might be just what the doctor ordered."

"Sorry to hear..."

"Sorrow not, Ed... what did you say your name was?"

"Edgar."

"Edgar. At my age if you can't appreciate the beauty of separation, divorce, broken love, being cheated on, and getting other various flavours of shit flung in your face, then, well, you're in for an ugly life. My theory is, there's no food without excrement. Get what I mean?"

"Uh, maybe."

"By the time it all goes down the throat and through the stomach and intestines, no matter how expensive the meal was or how pretty it looked on your plate, it always finishes as a brown tangy turd. Love – at least in my experience – seems to follow the same pattern. It always starts out looking real appetising and ends up de la merde , as the French say."

"Well, I'm kind of new at such things," Edgar said.

"Well, take your time, Ed. Who knows? Maybe one day there will be a new human digestive system on the market that will turn everything to gold. I've been thinking about that... about trying to find a way to turn things inside out. People get so stuck in their standard garbage... Anyway, nice hostel we've got here, isn't it?" the man Russ said.

"Yeah, nice people, great location."

"The girl at the desk said you might not be back tonight, is that right?"

"She did?" Edgar's underpants momentarily bulged like fish gills.

"Well, I'll hold down the fort. I flew in this morning and the jet lag is starting to kick in."

"Did she really say that?" Edgar blushed.

"I think she mentioned a dinner engagement. Something like that. Anyway, eat, drink, and be merry for tomorrow we shall die. Especially here. The food is wonderful. I was in France two summers ago with Cinderella and never in my life have I sensed the sensual like I did then."

"With...?"

"Actually her name was Audrey. She was my girlfriend until I found out I wasn't the only hot dog on her menu. Then she started being less of my girlfriend. Then I found out that not only did she like hot dogs, but she was an oyster freak, too. Then she started bitching about her freedom being compromised and she threw a dictionary at me. That was it."

"Sorry."

"Like I said, Ed, no sorrow, please. We're going to

turn this thing inside out." Russ the man hesitates, sits down on his bed and strokes his chin. "I'm telling you all this because you seem like a good listener. The girl at the desk told me what a nice guy you were. Actually it helps to think out loud. I'm going to get a story out of this while the soup is still warm." Russ the man pulls a bottle of Evian mineral water from a bag next to his bed and drinks. "So the way I figure it, maybe the solution is to start at the other end, that is, start with shit, send it up the digestive tract, and it'll finish coming out of the mouth looking like a five-star meal. Maybe we've got everything backwards. Maybe for love to work you've got to start at the bottom." Russ the man smiles, drinks some more, then says, "Hey, maybe I'm so full of shit that I don't even know what's up or down... How long have you been in Paris?"

"Just a couple days, but it seems like a lot longer."

"So you left your mission just like that?"

"I wouldn't say 'just like that'. I'd been thinking about all these questions about belief and truth and why we believe what we believe for a few years. Actually longer than that. As a kid I somehow sensed that everybody had his or her own story to tell, and that somehow they were all legitimate... or illegitimate, if you see what I mean?" Russ the man realises he has been talking more than his share so he nods and lets Edgar skip onward. "The church taught me to search for the truth. 'Know the truth and the truth shall make ye free.' I think that's how the saying went. The problem with the church is that if the truth you find doesn't agree with theirs then they say it's not the truth. For now the only truth I can come up with is that nobody has the slightest idea as to where the world – or universe – came from, if it has any reason to be, etcetera, etcetera. What fascinates me more than anything is how people do believe, and how they are basically satisfied with believing what their culture spoon-feeds them. Or if they decide to get off the ship, they usually jump on another ship that's even narrower than the one they were on before. Let's just say, I don't have a clue and, as far as I can tell, nobody else does either."

"Amen, brother," says Russ the man. Then a yawn slips from his soul.

"Well, I think I'd better take a shower," says Edgar.

"Cleanliness is next to godliness," says Russ the man.

"If only it were that simple," says Edgar.

"What's her name?" says Russ the man.

"Who?"

"The girl at the desk."

"Oh... it's Patricia."

"Bon appetit."

TWENTY-TWO

How do you like the foie gras? she said passing him another piece of toast.

It's good. I never liked liver, but this is different.

And the wine? It's a Chardonnay. One of my father's favourites. He loves his wine. He doesn't have a lot of money to buy the good stuff, except on special occasions. Then he always explains what we're drinking.

You know, it's all new to me, so I've got nothing to compare it with, but it tastes good. I like the way it's chilled.

The heater was on and the room was warm. Light came from the wires inside the heater and the candle on the table and her eyes.

Foie gras is a real delicacy for us. Some are better than others. This is a good one.

I got it across a bridge behind the Notre Dame.

You must have been on the Ile St. Louis. It's one of my favourite places. I don't understand why more tourists don't go there. Do you want me to give you a map?

That's okay. I kind of like feeling my way around, little

by little. If I stay long enough I'll figure it all out.

I haven't asked you. How long do you intend to be here?

I haven't asked myself. The missionary thing was to be for two years. I did five months. So there's a year and a half ahead of me with no real plans. The itinerary is empty. It's a funny feeling. I'd say it's the first time in my life when the future isn't more or less drawn up. At least the big lines.

What about the university? You said you have done how many years?

Two.

What were you studying?

Nothing in particular. You can do that in the beginning in America. I was mostly reading philosophy books because I had this religion and mission stuff so close to me.

Did you enjoy school?

Yeah. The first year I had lots of friends. I was doing all these projects to try to save the world. I thought if I was a Christian then my goal should be the same as Jesus's goal: save humanity. But then I realised if Jesus and his Daddy couldn't do it in two thousand years, my chances were pretty slim. Then I kind of disappeared into the library and read for a year.

She reached across the table and put her hand on the hand that wasn't holding the toast.

Most of the Americans I see at the hostel don't seem

too open to things. You know, here they are in France, and they're always asking me if we've got McDonald's and things like that.

You have to realise that most Americans really do think their country is the centre of the universe. Not only that, they think it's the only country God gives special protection to. When I was a kid my teachers used to say that God really did bless America. So God bless McDonald's, if you see what I mean.

It's rather amazing. We French are pretty bad, but not that bad.

The more I think about it, it seems it's just a logical extension of America being young and founded by lots of fanatical religious types. The religions haven't had time to get worn out like they have over here. Here you have a lot of nice old churches and people more or less ignore the Pope and all the rest and go about the business of living. In America religious leaders are basically new and they're all fighting to get on top of the totem pole. There's this all or nothing extremist tendency. Look at all the sects. Even the hippie movement is a kind of religion. The people in it have a religiosity about themselves, like they've got the answers and you and I don't. That's really the reason I wanted to leave America for a while. I got tired of everybody thinking they had all the secrets to the universe. The mission was a way for me to get away. The problem was that all the mission people had all the answers.

Was it hard leaving your family?

Of course it was. I cried. They cried. Or at least my mother did. But I have a tendency to like wherever I am, so I got over it pretty quickly. Once, when I was fourteen, I went to work on a friend's father's ranch in Montana. I cried all the way to the bus station in Oakland. When I finished the month on the ranch, I cried all the way from the ranch to the bus station in Helena, Montana. I don't know why, but I haven't yet met a place I didn't like.

You should come to the farm – I mean the golf course. The Jura mountains are special. Not like the Alps. They're more like rolling hills with lots grass and pine trees. It rains a lot though.

Did your parents try to keep you on the farm?

Not at all. They were absolutely in favour of letting their children do what they wanted to do. They made home nice, so the others stayed. I may live there one day. I don't know. I like Paris and so far Paris likes me. I haven't had any problems. I'm sure I'll travel some soon.

For the first time since he had known her, when she said this – so innocently – I'm sure I'll travel some soon – he realised that their togetherness might not last forever. He felt a rush of air shoot into his gut. Until then he had been so taken by their union, it had been so totally hermetic, that time had been completely absent. He had not for a second looked out of the bubble at what may lie ahead. Now he did. He wondered then how she saw it. Was he just part of the junk dangling from her road of time? He quickly swallowed his doubt, for then, anyway, and pulled the curtain back around the bubble. He was back in the small warm room. She went on talking.

I'd like to go to America.

This soothed him because he saw himself there.

A lot of French people – especially our age – say it's a cultural wasteland and all that, but I want to see the countryside, the parks, the canyons, the deserts. That's what interests me.

It is beautiful. What I've seen of it that is. Especially southern Utah and the area around the Grand Canyon and Lake Powell. My parents took us there one summer vacation a few years ago.

We never really took vacations. There were too many of us to fit in a car. But nobody seemed to need one. If you wanted a vacation you went for a long walk or you read a book. I did quite a bit of both. When we had the farm my father couldn't just up and leave the cows. You can't take days off from milking. Now with the golf course and the kids grown, maybe my parents will take a trip or two. Now that I think about it, other than going across the border to Switzerland, I don't think they've ever been out of the country.

Where would you like to go, other than America?

She poured Chardonnay.

You should probably ask where I wouldn't like to go? Iceland, Tahiti, Africa, Hong Kong, Australia. It doesn't really matter.

I'd like to go to Venice. I don't know why.

I would too.

He feels the curtains tightening round the bubble.

As a missionary were you just in Lyon?

Yeah. I could have eventually been transferred to another city, but I wasn't. Lyon and Paris are all I've seen of France.

So what did you do all day besides walk around and look for people to baptise?

Pray. Read scriptures. I was bad at both. I thought a lot. Mostly about the nature of belief. Why people believe what they believe. Why they believe at all. What is the motor behind belief. I started to think there were three reasons people believed. First, because of feelings. Their religion felt good. They got goosebumps in church or felt warm sitting around the Christmas tree singing carols. Whatever. Missionaries always talk about "feeling the Spirit". Well, as far as I can tell people all over the world "feel the Spirit" for all kinds of very diverse religions and causes. I'd try to explain this when I'd talk about my doubts, but nobody seemed to listen.

He sipped and when he looked at her he felt the Spirit.

Second, reason or logic. That is, what they think is logic. People build up a system in which everything fits in and so the system looks "logically" sound. No matter what happens in the world, the system absorbs it and reassures the person in his or her belief. "It was God's will" or "God is testing us" or whatever. In the Mormon church, like in all churches I assume, the people have answers for everything. Nothing falls outside their "logic" so the logic works to keep them believing.

She listened because she liked him.

The third thing is I'm starting to wonder if man's nature isn't to want to have something or someone to obey. If you look at the world and all the different religions, it makes me think that not only do people need answers as to why they are on Earth, but they need someone to obey while they are here. It's as if the need to be obedient is in the human genes. We've been obeying kings and priests and scriptures and police and parents for so long that we wouldn't know what to do if we stopped obeying. Look at kids who start disobeying their parents. What do they do? They get in a group and start obeying somebody else. They become hippies and join a commune or Hell's Angels and start dressing in black leather like the rest of the group. But whatever they do, they start obeying some other set of rules. I just started thinking about this, so I'm kind of thinking out loud.

Maybe you should study anthropology.

Maybe I shouldn't study anything.

Do you want any dessert? There's a little chocolate mousse left.

I'd love some. Maybe studying is just obeying a bunch of teachers.

Maybe making chocolate mousse is obeying my grandma's recipe.

She gets the chocolate mousse and delicately spoons it into two glass bowls.

How's your new roommate?

He's a nice guy. He used to be a basketball coach and now he wants to be a writer. He just broke up with his girlfriend. That's why he came to Europe.

Can he survive the night alone?

He said he was pretty jet lagged. He'll probably wake up at four.

And find you gone.

He knew about my dinner engagement.

Really?

Really.

They have talked until two. Patricia says I'm tired and goes over to Edgar's chair and places herself on his lap. She slowly swings both arms around his neck and licks the strands of chocolate from the corners of his lips. Her touch sends him soaring. They land on the bed and before the candle is out Edgar discovers what it is like to lie on one's back with puckered eyes and mould a mouth and plant seed after seed in another corner of the great garden.

TWENTY-THREE

When Edgar came back to the hostel near ten he found Russ the man in the breakfast room with his bowl of coffee and half a baguette.

"Hey, my long-lost roommate. How was dinner?" Russ the man said.

"Foie gras and toast."

"What?"

"Goose liver. I never thought I could eat anything with liver in it, but it was all right. What time did you wake up?"

"About three-thirty. But I fell back asleep around five. I'm fresh as a pig in a slaughterhouse."

"How's breakfast?" said Edgar sliding into a chair next to Russ the man.

"Well, a few minutes ago there were twenty screaming ten-year-olds in here. This is truly a youthful hostel. But they're gone and peace has been restored to the face of the earth. I'm a coffee-in-a-bowl kind of guy anyway and one of the reasons I got on the plane was to be able to eat a real French baguette. So I'm in heaven, Ed. Care to join me for breakfast?"

"I'm fine."

"So tell me Ed, why do you stay in the hostel if you don't use the bed and don't eat the breakfast?" Russ the man said winking.

"I'm not real sure..."

"I'm only kidding. I know a lot of guys who have two hotel rooms at the same time. I've got a couple friends in the NBA and from what I hear, they put Sally to bed at the Hilton and then go see Susie who's waiting so patiently over at the Holiday Inn. Love is a many splendoured thing... for those who can afford it and are six foot nine and look like they were sculpted by Michelangelo. So what's on your agenda today, Ed? Any special plans?"

"Not really. Not until this evening. My friend has classes until five-thirty."

"She's a student?"

"Yeah, over at the Sorbonne. But she works, too."

"How'd you meet her?"

"Checking in at the desk over there." Edgar gestures across the breakfast room.

"You rascal, Eddie."

"It just kind of happened. I don't know how. But she had something I'd never seen before in a person... a girl... a woman..."

"She's got more than something. She's got a whole batch of things from what I saw. Well anyway, I thought I'd start my vacation with a jog through Central Park."

"Is there a Central Park in Paris?"

"If there isn't, we'll find one, Ed. You want to come?"

"I haven't got any shoes other than my dress shoes."

"What size do you wear? I've got what I've got on and another pair in my bag upstairs."

"Eleven."

"I'm ten and a half. They'll fit, Ed. Let's go do the Paris marathon."

"I haven't got any sweatpants either."

"We'll figure something out. The first thing I do when I get to a city is go for a jog. It's like my way of acclimatising myself to a place. Once I've run around, I feel like I have a minimal sense of where I am."

"Okay, if we can find me some clothes, I'm in."

They went upstairs to the room and Russ the man emptied his suitcase on the top bunk. He outfitted Edgar with brown and orange sweatpants that said "AGGIES" on the side and a hooded sweatshirt that said "THE UNGRATEFUL LIVING" on the back. The shoes were a little tight in the toe, but otherwise fit like they had lived on Edgar's feet.

It was ten-thirty when they hit the Parisian macadam.

"Which way? I'm following you," said Russ the man at the corner of J-J Rousseau and St. Honoré.

"If you want a park, the only park I know is this way,"

said Edgar. So they crossed the street, ran to the Seine, then turned right toward the Tuileries Gardens. Edgar pointed out the back side of the Louvre.

"I went there with Cinderella," said Russ the man. "I think she fell in love with Venus from Milo. I think that's what her name was."

They went along the Quai de Louvre then cut into the park where the coterie of nude statues by Maillol was planted in a maze of bushes.

"Check 'em out," the man Russ said exhaling a cool vapor. "I'll come back later and see if any of them are free for dinner."

When they got to the Orangerie, Edgar huffed out a few sentences about Soutine and rain started to sprinkle from the sky. They crossed the Pont de la Concorde and ploddingly made their way up the Boulevard St.-Germain until they cut left on the Rue des Saints Pères and found the river again.

"How are you feeling?" the man Russ asked.

"Haven't run for a while, but not too bad. What about you?"

"I'm feeling like a beer when we get back to the stable."

"It's a good idea, this jogging."

"Beats a tour bus. I started doing it on our basketball road trips. Reduced the pre-game tension and got me out of the hotel rooms. And cities in Europe are even better because everything's usually so central. This whole place is like a museum for us American amateur globe-trotters."

"I've only been here three days, but it seems like a month."

"Shit happens."

The rain stayed a light drizzle giving a silver shine to the joggers' Paris. The showers in the hostel were also a drizzle. When they were dressed, shaved, and anointed, Russ the man invited Edgar for a beer at the bar next to the hostel. The beer was almost starting to taste good to Edgar. Russ the man drank his like it was gold and asked Edgar which he thought came first, God or beer. Edgar said he was weak in world history and Russ the man said that as far as he could tell beer was the best proof that God existed. Then he said that he used to say the first reason for the existence of sports is to have a beer after the game; the second reason is to have the beer with a friend; the third reason has yet to be discovered. So Russ the man drank another one. Then he said he was going for a walk. He did, back to the Louvre gardens and past the Maillol harem on his way to the Orangerie. He wanted to see Soutine's family for himself. Edgar wanted to take a nap.

TWENTY-FOUR

EDGAR CALLS HIS PARENTS AND CRIES

Before he went to Patricia's apartment that evening at six, Edgar decided to call his parents. When he had awakened from his snooze, they were there, with him, amidst his and his roommate's stuff in the semi-dark of the hostel room. His mother was crawling across his forehead saying, "It's up to you Edgar. You do what you think is right." His father was sitting in the chair next to the window telling a joke about a Mormon and a Catholic who go out duck hunting together. The Mormon takes his gun, his sandwich, and two bottles of milk. The Catholic takes his gun, his sandwich and two bottles of wine. They sit out by the lake for hours with nary a sign of a duck. They have lunch and the Mormon drinks his two bottles of milk and the Catholic drinks his two bottles of wine. Finally, at about four o'clock in the afternoon a lone duck appears in the sky. The Mormon grabs his shotgun and fires – BOOM, BOOM – but the duck keeps flying. The Catholic then takes one shot and down goes the bird. "Wow! How'd ya do that?" says the Mormon. "It's easy when there's a whole flock of 'em up there!" answers the Catholic.

Edgar goes to the post office to call. After much ado, he is able to place a collect call. It is five in the afternoon in Paris, so it's eight in the morning in California. The phone rings thrice. The charges are accepted.

Hello

Hi Mom this is Edgar

Edgar O Edgar we knew you'd call

I'm in Paris Did you get my telegram

Yes we did Your father's right here He's picking up the other phone in the bedroom We were just starting breakfast

Everything's okay I just couldn't continue The people were all nice the French and the missionaries But I just couldn't say we are right and they are wrong anymore

Where are you staying dear

In a youth hostel It's real nice It's right by the Louvre My roommate is a writer from New Mexico

We're so glad you called The Mission President called the morning you left Lyon and said you hadn't left a note or said anything to your companion but told us not to worry that these things have happened before

No I didn't want to get anybody involved It was my choice and wasn't anybody else's fault or anything

How did you get to Paris

I took the train at about five o'clock in the morning Everything is fine I hope you didn't worry too much Did

you tell anybody
> *Just your sisters*
> *How are they doin'*
> *They're teenagers*
> *Edgar*
> *Hi Dad*
> *Where are you son*
> *In Paris*
> *Paris Are you living with anybody*
> *I'm in a youth hostel It's nice It's a beautiful city*
> *So you're sure you are stopping your mission*
> *Yeah Dad I don't want you to think I don't respect all*

the teaching you've given me and everything but but I
just couldn't go on It wasn't fair to the church or myself
> *You're sure*
> *Yeah Dad*
> *Your mother and I have always respected you   we*

know you're good to people and always try your best
> *Th th thanks Dad*
> *O o Ed gar*
> *Th thanks Mo m m*
> *Have you told the Mission President where you are*
> *N n n o*
> *I think you should right away They feel responsible*

for you
> *I I I was just afraid they'd they'd they'd try to find me*

and try to convince me to to go on   and I just d d didn't
want to go through all that

Do you have any money son

A little And you gave me that cr cr credit card but I didn't want to use it unless unless I had to

When when do you want to come home

I don't know Mom Maybe in a couple we we weeks I need some time alone for a while

We love you son

I l l love you too Mom and Dad

Do call the Mission President

Okay D Dad I guess I better be g going Bye

Bye dear

Bye son

The tears in Edgar's eyes, as he softly lay the telephone on the hook, were tears of joy. There were not many parents like his, he thought. And maybe he was right. They had their beliefs, but they had the openness to allow someone else – even their own son – his. The monolithic monster hadn't eaten them like it had most Mormons he knew. His parents left a crack of light for another point of view. And he knew they knew that he was doing what he thought was right and that he had never tried to hurt anyone. Edgar's eyes dripped because he felt lucky.

The city spun around him. As he walked back to the hostel, the drizzle was now rain and it suited him fine. He was as warm as a nickel in a pocket.

Russ the man was sitting on the bed in his boxer shorts reading brochures.

"Where ya been?"

"I called my parents."

"Good move. Everything okay?"

"Yeah, everything's fine."

Russ the man sees the red at the eyes and says, "Hey, did you hear the one about the duck that goes into a store and walks up to the counter and says, 'Ya got any duck food?' (Edgar hasn't)

...Well, the guy at the counter says 'No, we haven't got any duck food.'

The duck walks out and five minutes later waddles back in, goes up to the counter and says, 'Ya got any duck food?'

'I just told ya five minutes ago that we haven't got any duck food!' the guy at the counter says.

The duck walks out, but five minutes later waddles back in, goes up to the counter and says, 'Ya got any duck food?'

'Listen, you stupid fucking duck, I told you we haven't got any duck food and if you come back in here again I'm gunna shoot you!'

The duck walks out, but five minutes later waddles back in, goes up to the counter and says, 'Ya got any bullets?'

'No!' screams the man at the counter.

'Ya got any duck food?'"

So Edgar tells Russ the man his father's joke about the Mormon and the Catholic and Russ the man smiles, and says, "I'd never heard that one before."

TWENTY-FIVE

How was school? he said as she set the steaming dish on the table. Her hands floated like feathers as she went back to the kitchen for the wine and napkins.

It was about Madame Bovary and Monsieur Sartre and how man is never satisfied. The professor, however, looked very satisfied, with himself, as he was expounding and his sheep were taking down his words. Actually he was pretty good. He said that we twenty-year-olds might not be quite ready to suck up Flaubertian soup because we haven't lived long enough to see our dreams turn to dust. At twenty, he said, you turn dust to dreams; the rest of life is watching the opposite happen. Good line anyway. This is another one of my grandmother's specialties. We call it gratin dauphinois. She says the garlic is the secret.

Grandma hasn't been wrong so far.

How about you?

I called my parents. They were nice. They just wanted to know when I was coming home.

And what did you say, she said scooping the potatoes onto his plate and kissing the side of his neck with her tongue.

I said maybe in a couple weeks but then I said we'll see because I need some time alone.

You call this being alone?

You know what I mean. Being away from the Mormon world.

Did they cry?

I'm not sure, but I did.

I would hope so. Otherwise I would classify you as an icy brute with no respect for his home, she said pouring the "Bourgogne ordinaire" that her budget allowed. Did you tell them where you were?

Yeah. I said I was in Paris. I told them I was in a hostel. I love them.

She sees the moist veil in his eyes that doesn't last as they eat the potatoes.

I went jogging with my roommate today. The showers in the hostel weren't as wet as the drizzle of rain.

Everybody complains and I tell them that if they are unhappy they can go bathe in the Seine.

Neither roommate nor I complained.

I didn't think so.

It was nice. He's a good guy.

He tells her the duck joke which she gets the second time around.

You know you can speak a foreign language when you

can understand the jokes, she says at the end of the laugh.

For dessert she had made a French plum pie. Then they went for a short walk down the Rue Vieille-du-Temple to the Hôtel de Ville, then back to the apartment.

Maybe you should move in with me, she said. I'll give you the same rate as you get at the hostel. I'm joking of course. This place costs me per month what you pay there in a week.

I might have to do it then.

Just promise me that you'll lift the toilet seat.

They sank to the bed and it happened again. They ate the apple, core and all. Before they fell asleep she turned on her radio and he heard Yves Montand sing *Le Temps des Cérises*. The angels were smacking into the walls like drunken birds.

So where do we go from here?

TWENTY-SIX

We move in.

We only have the one suitcase, so we don't ruffle the feathers too much. We put it under her bed. We hang our two suits on the coat rack.

We stay in touch with Russ the man by jogging with him every morning around ten-thirty. Sometimes we run towards the Opera, other days across the Seine, up the Boulevard St. Michel, and through the Luxembourg Gardens. Or we huff back through the Louvre and the Tuileries Gardens so Russ the man can flirt with Maillol's women. "If polygamy weren't dead," he says more than once, "I'd marry them all. And I'd be the first satisfied man since Adam."

"He was satisfied?" we ask innocently.

"He had to be. There was only one woman. He had nothing else to rattle his rocks about."

We usually finish with a sprint up the Rue J.-J. Rousseau and a beer or two after a shower.

"So how's life in the stable?" the man Russ asks one morning in mid-December as we water down with a couple Kronenbourgs.

"I'm a little like your friend Adam. Nothing to compare it to. For me it's a whole new ball game. She's introduced me to food, wine, painting, French music, all kinds of stuff we Americans have a tendency to miss out on. The truth is I love her to death. I could probably make love to her five times a day..."

"Why don't you?"

"Time, I guess. Or I fall asleep and forget to wake up in the middle of the night. She does work and go to school, don't forget."

"I forget what it's like to really want each other. Lately I've been in things where either I'm all over her or she's all over me, but never together at the same time. My symmetry has been a little askew. Can't seem to want the same dessert at the same moment."

"How's your writing coming?"

"No writing, just thinking. But the thinking is just as important as the writing. More so really. If the thinking hasn't been there the writing doesn't just show up. But I see why Miller and Hemingway and the boys came to Paris. You need an extra seven senses to suck up everything there is to suck up around here. I can't get over how civilised this city is – the food, the architecture, the public transport. You feel safe walking the streets after the post office closes. And the museums, galleries, parks. There's something about them. I've been here what? Two weeks? I haven't got any friends except you, but I haven't been lonely for a second. It's like the damn city's my friend."

"How much longer are you planning to stay?"

"Well, I said I'd been home for Christmas. How about you?"

"I called my parents yesterday and told them about Patricia and that I'd be going to her parents' house for Christmas. I figured they expected me to be away for two years anyway, so it should be okay. They said it was. I've never been farther east than Lyon, so I'd like to see the Jura mountains."

"You don't want to see the Jura mountains, Ed. You want to follow that smell of that pooh-pooh,"

"Pooh-pooh?"

"You know what I'm talking about."

"Well, then, both I guess. I do want to see where she lives."

The lady behind the counter flips up two fingers and Russ the man nods like the man he is and says, "Oui, s'il vous plaît."

"Hey, Russ, your French has quadrupled since yesterday."

"I'm working on it. By the time I get out of here, I might be able to conjugate the verb 'to be'. Je swi, tu swa, il swam, nous swimon. Ah, it don't matter, does it, Ed? I won't need it in New Mexico."

"You're the writer and literary man."

"So when are you going to her parents'?"

"A couple days before Christmas."

"Meetin' the in-laws, hey? I ended up liking my last girlfriend's mother more than I liked my girlfriend."

"They're pretty old. Patricia's the baby. They had her when they were about forty. Listen, I better get going. I promised I'd make lunch for one o'clock."

"What's on the menu?"

"I thought I'd show her what a bacon, lettuce, and tomato sandwich was. I've never seen one here."

"Too bad you can't find any Wonder Bread in this city."

"I'll make do without. See you tomorrow."

We go to our favourite little grocery store on the Rue du Temple. They have what they call pain toast to replace the Wonder Bread. When we walk in the tiny apartment Patricia is already back from school. She is bent over tying a garbage bag in the kitchen. "Just straightening things up so the chef can go to work," she says looking backwards with her head pointed to the floor.

"I'm going to make a great American specialty. It should be ready in ten minutes."

"How's our friend Russ?"

"We ran to the Place de la Concorde and back. He's leaving in a few days. I'll be sad to see him go."

"He told me yesterday at work. He said he'll miss his little brother."

What he didn't say was that he would have loved, more than anything in Paris, to get Patricia in bed with him. She had all the ingredients that made his stomach churn. But the man Russ did what might really make a man a man: he left her alone; he didn't try to fuck with his friend's girlfriend; he controlled the very difficult to control, not only because he liked Edgar and didn't want to risk destroying his first love, but because years before – fifteen to be exact – he had screwed a friend's girlfriend and swore he would never do it again. He had decided then that if there was one way for man to separate himself from the rest of nature's amoral jungle, it was by leaving friends' wives and girlfriends alone.

This is why we call him *Russ the man*, or sometimes *the man Russ*.

TWENTY-SEVEN

EDGAR GOES TO LES ROUSSES FOR CHRISTMAS

Before getting on the train for Les Rousses, Edgar took one last jog with Russ the man through the Tuileries Gardens and then back along the Seine. Edgar was in shape now and started feeling periodical adrenaline rushes. As they ran down the middle of the park, he sensed the thick billowed chrome sky sucking him inward and upward. But he looked down and his feet were still on the moist gravel-ground flapping next to Russ the man's. This day they ran in silence both knowing that their ritual was nearing its end. When they came back along the river towards Notre Dame, again Edgar felt as if he were to be taken into the heavens. Again he lowered his head and the earth was still his treadmill.

After the run, in the hostel lobby, they exchanged addresses and phone numbers. Russ the man told Edgar to keep the sweatshirt and sweatpants. He said Merry Christmas and that he would have preferred to be exchanging addresses with a lovely woman but that

Edgar had helped make Paris Paris. Edgar said that Russ the man had been just what he had needed to make the transition from the religious world to the pagan paradise. Russ the man said that maybe pagans and religious people had more in common than they thought they had and that one group just extended the future a little farther. Everybody was swimming towards something, he said. Or dog paddling, he said. They hugged, French-style, like a two-headed bear, and said goodbye.

Edgar went back to Patricia's apartment to take a shower. Patricia, dressed in a blue T-shirt, was packing her small suitcase when he opened the door. He unpeeled his wet clothes, put his underwear and socks in the sink to wash, and went behind the curtain in the corner that you pulled in a broken circle to make the shower. The water here also had trouble with gravity and wasn't much better than at the hostel. But Edgar had adjusted and didn't mind. Those gushing California showers were a thing of the past. As he was soaping, he heard the bathroom door open and Patricia come in. She pulled off her shirt and slipped behind the plastic curtain.

"I stink," she said.

"Like a perfume store."

They twisted, patted, and hummed. They rolled in the steamed garden and the fountain made a muffled pitter-patter as the seeds were planted anew. There were crickets, moths, butterflies, and a dove here and there, some in flight, others landed on the little cupboard, the sink, or on the peeling plaster walls. There were worms and ants and all sorts of crawling affairs watching and moving on the garden floor. The human blossoms rose and took their towels and wiped their skin warm. Then they stood before the book-sized mirror and they read the dots and lines around their chests. As they did, he told her the story he had read about Bertrand Russell, the English philosopher, who one day was talking to some nuns. He asked them why they bathed with their clothes on.

"Because we must keep our modesty in front of God," the nun said.

"But, my Sisters," Russell said, "if God can see through the roof, through the ceiling, through the walls and the door to the bathroom, what makes you think he can't see through your clothes?"

The train was at three-thirty, so they dressed quickly, closed up their suitcases, locked the door, and hot-footed it to the Metro at St.-Paul and to the Gare de Lyon just two stops away.

When they got to the station, the central hall was a thick herd of crossing, bumping, bustling people. Christmas, thought Edgar, more than any other season, sets mankind in motion. Patricia grabbed his wrist and pulled him through the thicket to quai fourteen. She knew the scene well. They boarded the train marked "Dijon, Dole, Vallorbe, Lausanne". They would get off in Vallorbe where they would be met by one of Patricia's brothers who would drive them to Les Rousses.

They plopped their suitcases on the overhead racks, settled into their seats, and Patricia whispered to Edgar, "First Christmas away from home, mon amour?" An unexpected chill went across his slightly damp back as he nodded and remembered the smell of his California living-dining room with chimney fire, decorated tree, and his mother bringing the turkey to the table for his father to carve. Patricia hugged his arm and he saw morning with the tree still lit and his pyjama-clad family coming in one by one to see and be the scene that is the joy of giving and receiving. "Thanks for inviting me," he said.

The train pulled out and Edgar fell asleep. Patricia read a few undigested pages of Sartre's "La Nausée", then switched to the magazine Mademoiselle.

They got to Vallorbe at ten twenty-two. It was snowing and nobody was on the platform to meet them. The station was small, dark, and ugly. It would have been uglier without the snow. They walked down some steps and under the tracks to the main entrance. The Buffet de la Gare and the kiosk were closed. An old man and an old woman were huddled together in the waiting room. They looked outside at a few parked cars and the silver-black-white of a snowy night. After a few minutes Patricia called her parents who said that her brother Paul had left an hour ago to pick them up. He should have been there. It must be the snow.

They went into the waiting room and assumed the same pose as the old couple. Patricia put her head on Edgar's shoulder using her scarf as a thin pillow. They held hands. A middle-aged man with a snow-wet hat came in a few minutes later. He went to the old couple. They rose laboriously and he hugged first the woman, then the man. "It's pretty bad out there," he said. "Sorry I'm late." They walked out, the middle-aged man in the middle holding a mother and a father's arm.

They waited until midnight when finally lights from a car could be seen through the window. They rose and went to the exit to greet Paul. But it wasn't Paul's car; it was the police. Paul's car had skidded off the road, down an embankment, and into a tree. He had been cut in the neck and had bled internally. When they found him, he had been dead for at least a half an hour, they said. The police told Edgar that this was the third tragedy in a week in the area. They told Edgar because Patricia couldn't listen because she was a prostrated tangle wailing on the floor just inside the station door. Edgar was on his knees next to her trying to hold her but she kept slipping out of his grasp like wet fish.

The police took them to the small hospital in Le Sentier where everybody would meet over Paul's body.

They got to Les Rousses at five in the morning. This was on the twenty-second of December. Christmas would not be a celebration of birth. It would be a death ritual instead.

TWENTY-EIGHT

EDGAR EXPERIENCES A FUNERAL AND WHAT GOES WITH IT

The funeral was quickly arranged for the twenty-fourth. A funeral on Christmas Day, it was decided by the less concerned, was full of too many contradictions. In any case, the local priest, Father Paré, had his hands full trying to explain a tragedy so close to the Christian celebration. He, nonetheless, laid out his logic: God had called Paul Tinguely back to Heaven because he had served his purpose on Earth; hence, the tragedy was not a tragedy, but a necessary step in God's plan. The Tinguely family didn't buy into this line of reason, but they let the priest talk and they let him set the funeral for the twenty-fourth.

Patricia seemed the most touched by her brother's death. Her parents had five other children and still harboured a dim hope that death was a beginning and not an end. Her brothers, now three, had seen so many cows die on the farm before it became a golf course that they, in silent fraternal unison, accepted the demise as part of nature's rocky road. Patricia, the last in the family line, had been somewhat shielded from the farm's gore and believed that what you see is what you get: a bloody breathless corpse is just that, i.e. a bloody breathless corpse that isn't going anywhere, except to rot in a stupid costly box under the ground. She cried for a day and when Edgar tried to console her she only cried louder. By funeral time she was so emotionally spent that she was the only family member whose eyes didn't drip a tear.

The church in Les Rousses is on the top of a small hill in the middle of the village just above a pizzeria and a butcher's shop. The immediate family, plus Edgar, were seated in the first two rows with the closed coffin three arms' lengths away. It was covered with flowers that Edgar wondered about: How were such fresh and beautiful flowers available in a mountain village when outside there was snow on the ground? Were they shipped in from Lyon or Paris? Did Les Rousses have a flower shop? Were they plastic? They couldn't be plastic, thought he, because the church smelled like a mouldy garden.

Given that Edgar had never met the person in the coffin, he had only the flowers and the copper box to look at. The people around him all had to suffer with the mangled vision of the person they had known as Paul. Edgar saw mostly roses – pink, red, and white. But there was also a large bouquet of yellow that he didn't know what to call. Dandelions? Zinnias? Chrysanthemums? Marigolds? He had heard these words come out of his mother's mouth back in California, but he didn't know what they corresponded to. Then he reckoned it didn't matter what they were called. They, like the rest of the flora, were there to somehow try to balance out the horror of a dead human body.

The priest entered in a long paper-white robe with gold trim. Behind him and the pulpit was a painting of Jesus on the cross. Jesus's head was tilted to the congregation's right and his eyes, though almost closed, peeked beseechingly towards the ceiling. Edgar wondered why God was always supposed to be up rather than down, but then he remembered that in Europe most such paintings were done before modern physics started telling people that we live in a universe that has no above and below. The priest put on his glasses and began what seemed to be a hastily put together speech about birth and death, Christmas and Easter, Christ and Paul (the deceased, not the apostle), God's grace, God's goodness, God's mysterious ways, and the wonderful truth that the deceased had probably already glimpsed the glorious gates of paradise.

The priest asked the group to rise for a prayer. Everybody did except Patricia. She sat unmoving, semi-slumped in her chair staring at the speaker. Her eyes shot cold flames. Edgar looked down at her and saw a young woman he had not known heretofore. Without returning his glance, she reached for his hand and squeezed it like it was a baby's arm. The prayer ended and the people sat down. Patricia turned her head toward Edgar's ear and in English said softly, "Fuck him."

The organ played.

Someone Edgar didn't know talked.

The organ played again.

Edgar sensed that the service was winding down when the priest took off his glasses. His tired thin eyes stared, as if at a damp trench, at the family. He reassured them, one last time, that they would meet Paul in the glory of the afterlife. He then pronounced a final prayer and instructed everyone to file out towards the front, to pass the family, but not to stop or shake hands. He invited the congregation to the cemetery, just out the north door behind the church, where Paul would be laid in his final terrestrial resting place. When Edgar heard the word "terrestrial" it brought him back to the Mormon explanation of the next world: the scum in the "telestial kingdom"; the in-betweeners plopped in the "terrestrial kingdom"; the good Mormons flouncing in the "celestial kingdom" where they live with God and even became Gods themselves.

The family members rose and waited for the shuffle of the congregation that obediently walked forward down the middle aisle, turned left, tried with a variety of facial and eyeball expressions to share the sorrow, did not shake a hand, and slowly exited. Edgar, following the pallbearers, the priest, and the Tinguely family, was the last one to leave the church. He turned and looked at the empty building. For the first time in his short life he sensed that apart from man's busy bustling, the universe is a cold place.

It was sprinkling snow as the group moved past the hotchpotch of other graves to the northerly corner where a rectangular hole awaited them. The priest and family walked behind the casket, followed by a broken line of loyal friends. The boxed body was set next to the hole. Paul would be the eternal neighbour of his grandmother, Bertha Jeanne Tinguely, 1889-1971, and his grandfather, François Deblue Tinguely, 1877-1953. The priest placed himself beside the casket and pulled a Bible from somewhere in his layers of frock. The family and Edgar stood to his right. Before he had read a paragraph, Patricia started to scream a scream that could only have meant death and it lasted. Her scream shut the priest up and she stopped only when her father and Edgar had dragged her out to the front of the church. It must have taken a minute. Each held an arm and she jerked. She squatted. She screamed some more. The bulk of the group had moved away from the grave towards her and her father and Edgar. She shook loose and ran down the hill towards the butcher's shop. Only Edgar followed. Before he could catch her, she slipped on the snow cutting her knee and ripping her coat. He tried to lift her, but she rolled and rolled leaving thin strokes of blood on the snow. She finally got up and screamed again, this time a French word, "connard". Then she collapsed, slithering limply out of Edgar's grasp onto the street.

The group arrived and Patricia was taken to her parents' house and put into her old bed. Her brother Paul was put into the ground before the priest could finish his speech.

TWENTY-NINE

PATRICIA GOES CRAZY AND GOES TO BESANÇON

She got what she wanted; she had shut the priest up. The son of a bitch was telling lies and she couldn't let him tell another one. Had she had a gun in her pocket, she probably would have plugged him gut centre as he stood over the freshly dug pit with the unholy black book in his cold rotting fingers. He would have reeled back a bit and then, trying to get a last grip on life, would have taken a couple steps forward and dropped like a lead statue into the open grave.

She hadn't had a gun, so she had screamed. Vocal bullets rising like sparks from her enflamed soul. You don't treat death that way. You don't denigrate a brother's life by prevaricating about his death. You don't paint a bloody dead rose lily-white and try to pass it off as a fucking valentine. You don't dress death in a tuxedo and a top hat and pretend it's going to a grand ball. No, you don't do that. Because when you do you strip life of the only value it has: its uniqueness, its facticity, its inscrutable temporality, the fact that it is what it is and nothing more and when it is gone it is... gone. She believed this because nothing had ever shown her that the contrary was true. She would have liked to believe otherwise, to have believed in a friendly frilled fairyland, but she couldn't. She had to believe that what is called "religion" is all lies. Spirit, soul, Heaven, Hell, good, evil, God, angels, afterlife, commandments, holy books, salvation, damnation – all untruths, all fabrications of the human imagination. Bad for our health. Bad for life.

And she believed that her brother's death should be about truth.

Patricia sputtered all this cold-tongued to Edgar only as she lay in bed the following morning which was Christmas.

When her parents and brothers came in to wish her well, she broke sentences apart and spat words. When the doctor came she mumbled and saliva overflowed from her mouth. When the psychiatrist came she screamed because something about him reminded her of the priest.

She stayed in the house for a week and then they gave her a shot and her parents took her to a hospital in Besançon. Edgar went too and when he kissed her goodbye at the door of her room she didn't really kiss, but reached down and finger-grabbed his belt and didn't want to let go. When she finally did, she turned and walked away towards her new bed.

THIRTY

Like some damaged duck wings, Edgar healed. It wasn't as if Patricia had left him for another guy. If anything, she had left him for a dead brother. And she didn't hop into another stud's bed. She hopped into a nuthouse. His pride was never put to the test of that of the jilted lover. Knowing what he knew about Patricia, i.e. her amazingly unique refined sensitivity to things physical, he thought he could understand how she had gone off the deep end. For all he knew, had Paul been his brother, he might have gone there, too.

She had told him – before they shipped her off to the hospital – to live in her apartment for as long as he wanted to. This he did, at first with great difficulty. The sights, sounds, and smells of the girl who had laid love in his lap perfused from every corner. She was nowhere, but everywhere.

He wrote her, but nothing came back. He tried to call, but they always said she couldn't come to the phone at that moment. He spent his days walking pavements, quais, and museums. His nights were at the table with bread and cheese and her radio. He wondered if he should go home. Finally after two weeks as a strayed neutered lamb, he decided life had to go on. In this case, his life.

But of course he had no idea as to what "go on" would mean.

He would start, like most do, by going out one night.

It was the seventeenth of January and it was cold. Edgar put on his brown sweater and overcoat and began walking towards Les Halles. It was around ten and there was a damp mist in the air that hung under the streetlights like a transparent beehive. When he came to the Rue St. Denis he turned right and ambled with a broken string of other lonely men toward the sex shops and peep shows. The farther he walked the more he wanted to peep. His gut contracted and skinny willie thickened in its tight cotton pouch. Most places advertised twenty francs which wasn't that much for a look at a living naked woman, so after two blocks up and one block back, he finally pulled a door. Sitting behind a small counter in a red-walled room was a thick man with an open purple shirt sitting in a high chair who greeted him with "What do you want?" Edgar wanted to see a living naked woman, but he didn't say as much. He fumbled in his pocket for some money, took out twenty francs and looked at the man.

"For that you get five minutes."

"Okay."

"For fifty you get a private show."

"Oh."

"For two hundred you can be in the same room."

"Okay."

"Is that what you want?"

"Umm."

"For eight hundred you can do it."

"I only have twenty."

He took Edgar's money and said, "Go through that door."

The door was dirty velvet and behind it was a series of stalls with nobody in them except now Edgar who sat down on a stool and looked through tinted glass at a small empty room with a chair in the middle. A few seconds later a woman about his age came in dressed in crimson: panties and brassiere. She evidently didn't know which stall Edgar was in because she kept looking at one two over from his. She sat in the chair and rather quickly removed her breast holder. Then she cupped each one a couple of times and moved her tongue across her lower lip which was puffy and graceful. Then she stood up and gyrated a little still glancing at a window with nobody behind it. Then she removed her panties. Edgar stared at her trimmed bush for a few seconds, until she did an about-face and walked out the door she had come in two or three minutes before. Edgar waited awhile thinking another girl might come. But nothing moved and he suddenly thought that in a place like this you might get mugged or molested, so he hustled towards the "sortie".

Back in the street he felt a wet drip on his thigh and wondered how it got there given that skinny willie had only slightly inflated with the girl's appearance and had wholly deflated as the show progressed and he definitely hadn't come close to anything as comely as come-come-coming into the soft wall of his underpants. Come Come Ye Saints he thought as he filtered back into the human stream on the skimpily neoned Rue St. Denis thinking about the enormous saga that was and is the education of the great American puritanical masses regarding skinny willie and sweet sally, and the beating of the brains that vainly try to beat back the planetary juices that keep life going. He thought of the drip on his leg and the body-brain brain-body connection that is probably understood by no one, yet professed by everyone, and how the world's morality masters have wrap-slammed tourniquet after tourniquet on skinny willies everywhere and have bashed brains with black-book bricks all in the name of gods that nobody has ever seen, heard, talked to, or played chess with on a rainy day in March. And he thought of all the sweet sallies worldwide that unwittingly produce the precious perfume that lures the poor slogged browbeaten skinny willies, like dogs to unwrapped baloney, only to have their sweet jewels chained to those black-book bricks and left to dry out like jerky on desert floors and have the priests and pastors call them good and pure and angelic while the soggy flustered enfeebled skinny willies of the world drip a sorry drop of come-come on a cold thigh. Come Come Ye Saints.

But the original Mormons had many wives and the male saints were able to shoot star after star at their sweet sallies who produced baby after baby and built the kingdom that spread over Utah, Idaho, Arizona, and parts of California and New Mexico, and Edgar's ancestors were told in 1890 that polygamy was no longer God's will because the American government threatened jail to the multi-wived and so the Mormons went back to monogamous monotony like the rest of America where maybe one in a million skinny willies is satisfied. But Brigham Young had had his twenty-seven wives, the lucky son of a bitch. Who wouldn't envy this American sultan who figured out how to turn puritanism into nothing short of a great orgy for himself and his teammates as they forged a civilisation in the Salt Lake Valley?

Edgar went into a café and had a beer. There were tourists and pimps and holy whores who, like him, were dying to live. They fingered their drinks and frowned and frolicked and took off their overcoats if they stayed for more than one. Edgar did, because had had nowhere else to go but back to a Patricia-less room in the Marais where he felt as lonely as an olive in an empty glass. He talked to no one until a fifty-year-old wearing a make-up cake

and a set-your-eyes-on-them-two-torpedoes dress top-
pled into the chair across from his and said "How are
you?" He decided for once to tell the truth which was that
here was an Edgar, shot like a streaming missile out of
California, planted in Lyon like a baby carrot, uprooted
and plopped into the streets of Paris, divinely wandered
into the Garden of Eden, Eve herded into a mental
hospital like a clown into a circus, now trying to heat up
his cold contracted skinny willie, sipping a pastis with a
coterie of Soutine's friends, thinking about the ways of
the world and the girl in and out of red that he peeped at
leaving him hardly half a step past where he had started
in this frozen January night. Amen, brothers and sisters.

How much you got?

If I told you you'd laugh.

No I wouldn't because I'm an angel.

I've already met one angel tonight.

Could she fly through windows?

Nope.

Could she make a pickle dance?

What?

I said could she make a pickle dance?

Are you a poet or an angel?

The one doesn't preclude the other honey?

Okay she couldn't.

Some can't.

She lifts a boot under the table and tenderly presses it
against Edgar's leg. One thing leads to another and the

next thing you know, for the price of a cup of coffee, sweet sally is squeezing skinny willie like a jellyfish its dinner.

THIRTY-ONE

Before March came Edgar found himself a job to at least cover Patricia's rent. He washed dishes lunches and evenings in a Chinese restaurant just around the corner from the apartment. They threw in a meal a day which helped, too. Edgar was free from three to six and as the weather got warmer he started walking or jogging over the Seine to the Luxembourg Gardens during the break. If the sun was out he would sit and read. If not, he would keep moving.

He had spoken to Patricia once and she said what he expected her to say, to wit, that the hospital people were the crazy ones and that she was the only one with a light on upstairs. Unfortunately this didn't work in her favour for getting out. She said she might soften her tone. She told Edgar that she still shouted obscenities every time she saw anything or anyone associated with the clergy. "I'll do my best to be out by Easter," was the last thing she said.

It was the twenty-fifth of March when Edgar lowered himself into a green metal chair next to the round fountain on the north side of Paris's famous garden. Spring was pushing past the winter air and the sun lay softly on the shallow water. He pulled a used copy of Camus's "La Peste" from his jacket pocket, but he didn't feel like reading about the miseries of the planet or morality in the face of a deaf universe. Instead, he decided to think alphabetically:

A for apple. An apple, any apple, Edgar's apple, is an incredible fucking miracle. But we are too blind to see it. That an apple simply "is" should be enough to flip us into a loony bin. But we're too obtuse. Does an apple require a maker? A God? Does God require a God behind Him? If a God can be uncaused, why can't an apple be likewise?

B for bullshit. Bullshit, horseshit, cowshit, dogshit, manshit, womanshit, omnishit. Slinging it is easy. It's wiping it up that's hard. It gets flung on the mind and congeals, like toothpaste in a sink. Except that it takes centuries to get cleaned up. And even then... Nobody wipes it up. It cakes, coagulates, and we corrode. We're stuck in it, can't lift a foot out of the crap that people have been saying, thinking, and believing for centuries.

C is for care. I say I care about all life. I want the best for everything and everybody. But it doesn't work. I have to eat. There will always be the eaters and the eaten. So much for morality. I can only care so much. Otherwise I go crazy because there are, will be, and always have been losers in life's rusty chain. If I don't limit my care, care will blow my mind.

D for death. The one certainty. Hence any philosophy of life should be based on death. Death as a starting point. Now what do we do with life? Knowing death is there, waiting – like a hawk circling, cruising an opaque azure sky with eyes tugged downward towards an eventual prey – to open its wings and carry me and everything else with it into the coming night, I live. This knowing death is maybe the only thing that can make me see life differently. Death as the telescope through which we can see past our clogged noses.

E for Edgar. The name that I associate with me. You have yours, I have mine. Ugly, this name of mine? Maybe, but always sweet on soft lips. It has always been mine and always will be mine. Edgar and I are one, but are not equals. Like God and Jesus. For the I always posits the Edgar.

F for fuck. Such a crucified word. Nature's loveliest and most necessary act beaten to a pulp by society's moralists and blasphemers. Males and females everywhere juicing up, then wittingly combing the earth for a partner, for one with whom to blend, if even for a short moment, such that the juices find their way out and in and the juicing begins anew. The whole universe fucks in one way or another. Universe and fucking are almost synonyms, yet we treat the one with cosmic respect and the other like a dirty sock.

G for God. If one thing is clear it's that He, She, It or Them ain't. Ain't clear, that is. And "G" for guilt. Can there be guilt without God and vice versa?

H for home. I will go home. I will make home. The word gives me goosebumps. Pigeons have homes. Mice have homes. Dogs have homes. I have made Paris my home. When I leave and come back and smell her groin, I will know where I am.

I for I. Why is it not capitalised in French? Do the French know something we don't know? That maybe the "I" isn't as big and strong as we think it is, that it's more of a little "je" fluttering around like a "you" or a "he" or an "it", waiting for that circling hawk to carry it off to nothingness.

J for justice. There is none. Why can't we admit it? Of course we need laws, goals, and myths. But "Liberty and Justice for All"? Come on. We can do better than that. All what? All people like you and me? But nobody's like you and nobody's like me. Laws for all, okay. But justice? Liberty? If we can't know what makes a man what he is, we can't talk about administering justice. And we don't know what makes a man what he is. Only God knows because God is omniscient. That's why everybody pretends they're tuned into God. So they can judge and administer their phony version of justice and they can quack about liberty for all. People who have the goodies or want the goodies talk about justice and freedom. People who look at the truth of the distribution of the goodies know that their distribution is like the weather: rain here, snow there, drought here, blue skies on that corner, thunderstorms on this. No liberty, no justice. Just a big swirl that keeps swirling.

K for knowledge. Oh Edgar, you have thought about this, but not enough. You like knowledge, you learn names of painters and poets and presidents, and you learn how to make a cake or build a bridge or a bomb, and you want to call this knowledge. So you do. But like you build knowledge, you can also destroy it. You can say that to know a name is to know nothing about what the name represents, that behind the name is an infinity that you will never fathom. You can build a bridge, but you will never know all who cross it. You can build a bomb, but you will never know who the bomb hit and how the flesh tore and the mind went berserk. You might know this, but you will never know that. And even the this is always on the mind's own terms. And what about the great inflated Socratic imperative, "Know thyself"? If there is one this that I can't know, it is myself. To know myself I would have to know the brain that is doing the knowing. And this I can never know because I cannot know that which is doing the knowing. I can only know the result, what my mind thinks it knows. K for knowledge? Maybe K should be for K-Mart?

But so what? Because L is for love. "Lovely little Lucy is licking a large lollipop." L is for love. Lucy's love. Larry's love. Lamar's love. Linda's love. All different, of course, but all lumped together under one word. But maybe the heat in the body or the tightness in the throat or the longing for the loved are as universal as blood. Forget the types. We all have it. Blood and yearning make us all brothers. What I feel for Patricia all men feel. The hole in me that only she can fill. For a while. Until there is a new hole. And what about love, not for our lover, but for our neighbour? What of this? Love thy neighbour as thyself, they say. But who loves himself? Who even knows how? What might self love look like? How would it dress? What would it eat? What perfume would it sprinkle on its neck? What would it do after lunch? Would it go back to work or take a nap? Would it try to make millions or try to write poetry? Would it buy a new car and get regular dental check-ups? Would it walk when it's easier to drive? Would it say "I love you" to the helpless asshole? Would it continue to sit in this green metal chair or would it rise and go find a needy whore for a needy skinny willie? Or would it go to church and give alms? Can you love another if you don't love yourself? Can you love yourself? Lick the lollipop lovely Lucy until the last sugary lump has left the stick bare.

M is for motion. I have a sneaking suspicion that the whole universe, like Paris, is constantly in motion. Even the sleeping are moving. The dead are decaying. Electrons fly constantly. Nothing is fixed. We just like to pretend things are. So we can love them. Like me and Patricia. I thought she would always be that woman that took me to her room that night and wrapped me in the cosiest blankets of bliss. But no, she is no longer there for that. Motion has moved all that. I move as I sit, off to another thought like a melting cloud.

N for nature. Nature, you say, is what is natural. Like trees and flowers and bees and beehives. But what about men? You say they are not natural when they build steel buildings and smoky factories. But why is this any less natural than the bees and the beehives? Because it pollutes, you say. But why isn't pollution natural? I say. Because it is man-made, you say. Oh, I say, bee-made is natural and man-made is not natural? Very interesting, I say. Man is natural, but what man makes that pollutes or is ugly is not natural, I say saying what you say. Think again, I say. If you ask me, I say the whole universe is as natural as an ice cream cone after church.

O is for omelette. I hate eggs. Always have and don't know why. The cracked shell. The yellow suns afloat in the pan stirred until mushy hard like hot discoloured cotton. Maybe that's not even how they're made. I don't look at what I hate. I only imagine from old kitchen smells and seeing the result steaming as my mother softly shovels with wooden spatula to my father's plate. Oh well. If I must hate let it be an omelette. They made me try it, but seeing me gag as hand flew to mouth, never made me try it again.

P for pussy. Were Edgar a woman would it be for prick? But he is not and his half of the universe fights wars, climbs mountains, crosses seas, and walks deserts to get to the sweet velvety swinging doors which, when opened, reveal the little moist honeyed pussies. Now Edgar knows, thinks he on the green chair next to the fountain watching mummies watching their children sailing boats, what turns the cogs of the great wheels of life. Something must turn them. Since he found Patricia, and, with the ease of a cat licking milk drops from a paw, found the floppy doors that opened to her pink treasure, he has sensed that pussy is at the heart of most male prayer. We want food and warmth and goods and success, but all are an extension of the tiny lake of love that is the pussy.

Q for quilt. His mother made him a small one before he was old enough to start school. It was bluish plaid with bits of white and red and it went to bed with him every night even after it no longer covered his growing body. It then would cover a neck and a shoulder. It smelled of milk and what he hoped was his own smell because that smell he would want to share with others. Until he was five he dragged it with him in the house in clenched fingers leaving a free thumb to enter his mouth. He took the thumb out to talk or to play. He dropped the quilt only to play. His quilt was a person if we're talking about what really happens.

R for rain. Edgar stopped complaining about rain the day he realised that our world needed it. It's that simple, he thought. Without water, no world. So why do we bitch about it? We're so stupid that we call rain bad weather. But without it, we wouldn't be here to bitch.

S for sun, not sex. Sun and rain are blood brothers. The Aztecs knew what to worship. None of these anthropomorphic monstrosities bent on trying to explain why we're such unappreciative assholes. Or trying to stretch our pathetic little ephemeral selves into eternal glory mongers. Or trying to babysit us through life to keep our hands off our neighbours' cookies and our polished pricks caged like circus animals. No. No. Let us kneel before the sun. The Sun. A real God. A three-lettered god we can't live without. We haven't refined our gods; we've rotted them. We've stopped worshipping life and started throwing our souls and pennies at imaginary Santa Clauses.

T for time. It's four-fifty. I have to be to work at six. Washing the sticky sweet and sour sauce off the dragon-faced plates at Kwong Ming's Chinese diner. Human time. My time. Time to get up. Time to take a shower. Time to say goodbye. Time to call home. Time to clean your room. Time to brush your teeth. Time as we know it. Slow, grinding, ticking, then taking off like a dog after a fox as we hit a pleasure zone or look back to the day before yesterday. Napoleon's time. Kennedy's time. Edgar's time. Only we count the days.

U for United States. Edgar thinks of his country with love and affection. He has been away from it for more than six months, long enough to realise that it is one among many. It holds souls. France holds souls. China holds even more. Like his blue quilt held his. Let

Americans believe they are the best. Let everybody believe they are the best. Let everybody think God is blessing them. Don't ask questions. God bless America, goddammit. It don't matter that today's Americans were yesterday's French, Swiss, English, Germans, Italians, Africans, Chinese, Mexicans, Vietnamese, etc., etc.. This don't matter none. Today we'z Americans. One nation under God with liberty and justice for all. Thank goodness we set those slaves free and stopped shootin' them Injuns.

V for victory. Ever since he was in junior high school Edgar has realised that one man's victory is another man's defeat. Most of the time anyway. Should we invent new games? Should we boo the victors for screwing up the losers? Should we crush the losers even more? Should we send the losers to the White House? Should we stop playing games? Should we just laugh a good laugh?

W for wish. When you wish upon a star, it makes all the difference who you are. Or does it? Edgar is wishing that tonight Patricia will be waiting for him when he gets home after work smelling of monosodium glutamate and spring rolls. The world is a wishing well. And she won't be there.

X for x-ray. Edgar remembers the fuzzy picture that was his arm before they threw on the cast that went around his elbow and almost to his armpit because his neighbour tripped him in a street baseball game and when he got up the broken bone was peeking at him through the skin. It hurt his mother more than him when she saw it and they got in the car and rushed to the hospital. But that was...

Yesterday. One of Edgar's favourite words, not because of the Beatles, but because it implies the peace that things are done, that another day has been put to rest, another night of sleep laid like a cushion between now and then. Edgar realises that his yesterdays are not sharp nails that puncture his todays. He is lucky. They are warm slippers that protect his feet for tomorrow. They are posts in the water that hold up the bridge.

Z for zero. o. Zer – o. Round like the breast and the nipple that he sees as he lifts himself from the green metal chair and begins walking to the western gate of the Luxembourg Garden. No, Patricia won't be there that night. But she has been there. And she might be there again.

As Edgar gets to the exit he meets an elderly woman being tugged, leash in hand, into the park by a lively beige Labrador. She cocks her head sideways trying to keep her balance, looks at Edgar, produces a slightly exasperated smile, and says, "Mon Dieu!"

ABOUT THE AUTHOR

www.jonfergusonbooks.com

More Huge Jam titles by this writer:

The Anthropologist
Nietzsche for Breakfast
Adam's Cane
Foster's Depression
The Flood
The Old Man & the Stone
Three Forgotten Tales
The Last Day Forever
The Burnt Roses
Don't Bullshit Me Daddy
Don't Bullshit Me Johnny
Don't Bullshit Me God

... and more publishing in 2025!

From *Nietzsche for Breakfast* by Jon Ferguson:

'The fact that man is and has been around for a while does in no way mean that he holds the keys to what the world really is. Fish, goats, geese, and bacteria have probably shown equal or greater longevity and surely no one is going to venture that they "know" what "is".

'Nietzsche wants to put man in his place — wherever or whatever that may be. He wants us to stop deluding ourselves; if we don't or can't know what the world really is, let's face the music and at least dance in the dark with a well-lit conscience.'

M C Gardener's review of *The Anthropologist*, preceded by an extract from that novel *(anotheramerica.net)*:

"*I had intended to talk to you today about Edmund Leach, the famous English anthropologist... But as I was walking to campus this morning, I decided to talk about somebody else who, contrary to Leach, is never discussed in academic circles. His name is Juan José Carlos Rodriguez. He is a gardener here on campus. Yesterday he was planting pansies along the walkway outside the building you're sitting in. I decided to talk about him instead of Sir Edmund Leach because he has been more of an influence on my thinking than Leach has. I don't say this to diminish the importance of Leach, but to amplify the life of Juan José Carlos Rodriguez.*"

This is the beginning of the 'Rodriquez Mediation.' It appears at the beginning of chapter eight approximately midway through the book. Fuller will employ Rodriguez in the denouement of the mystery of the red hair in the book's final pages. That denouement is a delightfully absurdist conclusion to a fine novel. I will leave it to the reader to discover it and the second half of the book... It is as abundantly rich as the first and concerns itself with second narrative strand to which I earlier alluded. The 'Rodriquez Mediation' takes up the whole of chapter eight and is among the finest half dozen pages that the author has penned. Initially it is simply one man's story. But no matter how simple the man no man's story is simple. Rodriguez's story is one of tragedy and strength – it is a tale of the earth by a tender of the soil. Fuller narrates it as it was narrated to him some twenty years before. Its force and loveliness is one not diminished by time.